Praise for Cassandra Dean

I fell in love with this book from the first bewildering, smoldering scene, and was captivated until the last page.
– The Romance Reviews

With just a whisper, a caress, or a simple kiss, Ms. Dean takes the reader on an adventure full of hedonistic pleasure as well as bittersweet moments.
– Coffee Time Romance

Be prepared to experience a wide range of emotions. I found myself laughing, crying, blushing and even yelling at times.
– Romancing the Book

Cassandra Dean
Stealing Lord Stephen
Lost Lords, Book Three

STEALING LORD STEPHEN
Copyright © 2022 by Cassandra Dean
Print version: Copyright © 2022 by Cassandra Dean

Cover Design: SeaDub Designs
Interior Book Design: SeaDub Designs

Editing: White Rabbit Editing

All rights reserved.
No part of this publication may be reproduced, distributed, or transmitted in any form by any means, including photocopy, recording, or other electronic or mechanical methods, without the prior written permission of the publisher, except in the case of brief quotations embodied in critical reviews and certain other non-commercial uses permitted by copyright law.
This book is a work of fiction. All names, characters, locations, and incidents are products of the author's imagination. Any resemblance to actual persons, living or dead, locales, or events is entirely coincidental.

By Cassandra Dean

Enslaved
Teach Me
Scandalous
Rough Diamond
Fool's Gold
Emerald Sea
Silk & Scandal
Silk & Scorn
Silk & Scars
Silk & Scholar
Silk & Scarlet
Slumber
Awaken
Finding Lord Farlisle
Rescuing Lord Roxwaithe
Stealing Lord Stephen

To everyone who waited patiently

CASSANDRA DEAN
Stealing Lord Stephen
LOST LORDS, BOOK THREE

Prologue

WHEN LADY SERAPHINA WALLER-MITCHELL was two months old, her mother handed her care to a nursemaid and sailed for Rome. Having secured funding for her latest expedition with her marriage and her womb, the Marchioness's passion for archaeology and antiquities far outweighed the negligible delights of motherhood and she gave no more thought to the daughter she left behind. The servants didn't know what to do with an infant, however they did their best to manage the newborn daughter of their lord.

Seraphina's father, the Marquess of Tidswell, had left for Ceylon many months prior to his daughter's birth. He did not much care for his new wife, having reluctantly acquired her only to secure the future of a marquessate he'd never thought to inherit. The third son of a third son, he had spent most of his life amusing himself with a plantation secured by his long-deceased father and was eager to return once the wedding and bedding had been done. Not even when the news eventually reached him that Marchioness had borne only a girl child, and thus he had no heir, had he been tempted to return.

When Seraphina was seven, a letter from Rome arrived advising of the death of her mother. Seraphina hadn't been sure if she was sad. She'd known she should be—her mother was dead—but it was difficult to mourn a person she had never met. She had done her best, though, and Mrs Middleton, the housekeeper, arranged for her clothing to be dyed black and similarly hued wreathes hung on doors. Many people Sera didn't know sent condolences, the spiky pen marks blurring before her eyes. She could not read some of the words, and though she was making her way through the books in the library, she was still only seven and her vocabulary—she was proud she knew what that word meant—was not fully established. She knew this to be as Miss Webster, her governess, said it often.

With the death of the woman he'd married, the Marquess finally decided to return to London. He sent word ahead and Seraphina spent the time between the letter's arrival and her father's in a state of nervous excitement. Finally, she was meeting her *father*. Someone who would laugh and toss her in the air and give her lemon drops, as she'd seen Ned the groom do with his daughter. Her father would read her bedtime stories and she would let him, even though she had learnt to read ages ago. She would finally have a family, and her father would stay and care for her and life would be grand.

The day of her father's arrival, Seraphina wore her best dress, her finest slippers. Her nurse had spent a half-hour brushing and arranging her hair, weaving a ribbon into a complicated half-braid. Gaze trained on her bedroom door, she sat rigid on her bed, not daring to move in case she mussed herself. Finally, the door opened and John the footman bade her attend her *father*.

She followed John, tugging at her fingers until they reached the study. John rapped on the door and a firm voice bid them enter.

She had not often been in the study, only when Sir Walter, the solicitor in charge of her trust, came for his quarterly checks. Sir Walter occupied the study now, but instead of sitting behind the desk as he usually did, he stood awkwardly by its side. Instead, a man she had never before seen sat behind the desk.

Joy filled her. This must be her *father*.

He appeared like any other man, though he was dressed in clothing that seemed exotic, with bright colours she had only seen ladies in the park wear. He had no moustache like Sir Walter, or a beard like Charlie, Peter or Xavier, the grooms.

The man—her father—looked to the side. "*This* is my daughter?"

"Yes, my lord," Sir Walter said.

Her father sighed. "I suppose she'll do." He crooked his finger. "Come here, girl."

She took careful steps toward him, determined to impress

him with what Miss Webster had taught her. From behind the desk, he assessed her. She tried not to be disappointed he did not immediately hug her. Perhaps he felt a bit funny. She felt a bit funny when she met new people.

"You have my look, I suppose, but your hair, that must be your mother's."

Abruptly, she was ashamed of the hair she and her nurse had spent so long attending.

"Do you attend school, girl?" her father continued.

"No, sir. Miss Webster teaches me."

"Miss Webster?" he said to Sir Walter.

"The governess, my lord."

Her father scoffed. "She will attend boarding school."

Sir Walter appeared confused. "But she is the daughter of a marquess, my lord," he said. "Is that wholly appropriate?"

"It is appropriate if I say it is appropriate."

Seraphina looked between Sir Walter and her father. Neither of them looked at her. "But I don't want to."

Her father's gaze whipped to her. Frowning, he said, "You will do as I say."

"But I want to stay here, with Miss Webster and Mrs Middleton and Ned and John and Peter."

"Servants," her father said with disgust. "You must be amongst your own. I will direct my secretary to make the arrangements."

"But, Father—"

"You will be going and that is final." He turned to Sir Walter. "Where are those titles for the Marchioness's property?"

Seraphina stared at her father and, horribly, she couldn't stop the tears that welled. Angrily, she scrubbed at her face and dipped into a curtsey.

"Yes, Father." Maybe if she agreed he would give her a lemon drop.

Her father looked up, surprised. "You are still here?" Waving a hand, he shooed her away. Not knowing what else to do, Seraphina did as he bade and left the study.

Two days later, a footman escorted her to a carriage and she was taken to Robertson's Finishing School for Ladies. She did not see her father again, and only a short missive from Sir Walter four months later advised her he had returned to Ceylon.

When she returned home for Christmas, the servants who had been her family had been dismissed. Strangers had taken their place, and she spent her holidays alone.

She did not return home at Christmas for the rest of her time at finishing school.

Seraphina had been at finishing school for four years when a new girl started. This new girl was small and alone and reminded Seraphina all too much of herself, when she had been weak and small and her father had deemed her unworthy. Every time Seraphina saw the new girl, she felt uncomfortable and agitated, and she *hated* that this girl made her feel so.

One day in the dining hall—it was a Tuesday, she remembered that detail quite clearly—she could take no more of this feeling.

"You!" she hissed.

From across the communal table, the new girl looked up.

Seraphina had no desire to learn her name. "I find I do not wish to rise from my seat. Prepare a plate of dinner for me."

The new girl gaped at her.

Seraphina exhaled impatiently. "You are quite useless, aren't you?"

"I—"

"Make yourself useful. Fetch the plate."

"I—"

"I—I—" she mocked. "Can you not speak?"

"I—" The new girl blanched.

Seraphina laughed. "You cannot speak," she said, clapping her hands together. "How delightful. Nonetheless, you do not get a say in this. You cannot speak and so you shall do as you are told. You will prepare a plate for me, for Maria, and for Elizabeth, and you will bring them to our table."

Frozen, the girl stared at her with wide eyes.

"Well?" Seraphina said. "What are you waiting for?"

The girl started, and then scurried away.

Maria and Elizabeth tittered. Sera lifted her chin. She felt…better.

After that, she often ordered others and found, to her surprise, others would obey her. Soon, she arranged everything to her liking, and those who didn't adhere to her liking she punished. Rumour and innuendo become her weapons, and so too a sharp tongue with wicked words. In the world of the finishing school, all girls quickly learnt not to cross her.

When she was seventeen, preparations began for her debut to society. She returned to Tidswell House in London, dismissed the servants her father had employed and engaged her own. Her debut was made with the proper pomp and ceremony, and she dedicated herself to ensuring she controlled it as she had her boarding school.

Life continued, as it always did. If, after eight years in society, life felt a little duller, a little less fulfilling, well Seraphina would discover a new way to amuse herself. Another year loomed, and she prepared herself as she always did. Perhaps she would tempt a man to ruin, perhaps she would toy with a debutante. There were a myriad of options, and each would quiet the voice in her head that whispered she was unworthy. This year would be like all the others.

And that voice would remain silent.

Chapter One

London, England
July, 1819

THE CARRIAGE JERKED OVER a bump in the road. Righting herself, Lady Seraphina Waller-Mitchell laced her fingers and stared straight ahead, her mind ticking over every step she would take that night.

She had no cause for nerves. This ball would be no different from any of the hundreds of balls she'd attended before. Indeed, she arranged each to her satisfaction, ensuring all would progress as it ought.

She would alight from her carriage and make her way to the entrance hall where she would be announced by the Pruitts' majordomo. Maria and Elizabeth would then attend her, having arrived at the ball prior to her as instructed. They would proceed to the southwest corner of the ballroom, which had the best aspect, and she would set up court, selectively choosing from those in attendance to provide amusement. She would bestow ten of the fourteen dances on six suitors of her choosing, forgoing four to instead observe and comment, and she would allow another suitor to bring her delicacies and punch. Elizabeth and Maria would relay the latest gossip, and from those in attendance she would determine on whom she would focus her efforts and her condescension. She had her strategy for a successful ball attendance and it would work, as it always did.

The carriage shuddered to a stop. The door opened and

Jim appeared, the footman holding out his hand. "Good luck tonight, my lady."

Sera placed her hand in his, gathering her skirts in the other. "I don't need luck, Jim. I have a plan."

His lips twitched as he helped her descend. "Of course, my lady."

Setting her foot on the gravel, she sniffed. "Don't be impertinent, Jim. I should hate to have to terminate your employment, and it will do you no favours at this time of year. It would be next to impossible to find another position at this late stage, you know."

"Yes, my lady," he said mildly, as one who was often threatened with such and knew the threat to be completely toothless. Jim had been in her employ these eight years past, and she threatened to disengage him at least once a week.

To keep up the façade, she sniffed and then sailed into Pruitt House.

She had arrived almost two hours after the stated time on the invitation, as she had always intended, and thus the event was now a crush. Anyone who was anyone knew to arrive late was an absolute must, and she always added an extra half hour to ensure she was one of the last to arrive. People spilled from the ballroom into the entrance hall, down the corridors towards the cards and retiring rooms. Already the din was excruciating, the noise of hundreds in too small a place overwhelming.

Excitement stole the breath from her lungs. Finally, apprehension waned and she let the ball wash over her.

The majordomo stationed at the threshold to the ballroom nodded as she approached. "Lady Seraphina Waller-Mitchell," he announced.

His proclamation drew little notice from the crowd. Lifting her chin, she swept into the throng. It did not matter that she did not draw notice. She would, as always, make them notice.

Conversation and laughter melded into a cacophony, accompanied by the strains of the orchestra. The dancing had not yet commenced, ladies gossiping behind their fans while gentlemen pretended they did not listen in earnest. Lady Pruitt had chosen a Greek theme for her ball, with marble columns and drapery. Grottos had been created from columns and greenery, the most elaborate housing the orchestra. The grotto with the next best vantage stood on the other side of the ballroom and was already occupied. Four young girls, debutantes all, whispered and giggled where Sera had planned to be.

Annoyance drew her brows. Elizabeth and Maria had been under strict instructions to reserve the grotto with the best vantage. Stern words would be exchanged once she rectified the situation.

Arriving at the grotto that should be hers, Sera arranged a pretty smile on her features. "Good evening."

The girls stopped talking. "Lady Seraphina," one exclaimed.

Regally, she inclined her head. "My dears, I find myself confused as to why you have taken occupation of this area of the ballroom."

They glanced amongst themselves. One of them said hesitantly, "Lady Seraphina, we thought—"

"This grotto is not to your best vantage," she interrupted. "You would do well to remove to the eastern corner of the room, close to the orchestra. The gentlemen always gravitate that way."

They glanced at each other excitedly. "Oh, thank you, Lady Seraphina, thank you."

"Of course, my dears. Only too happy to help."

Breathlessly talking amongst themselves of which gentleman would take note of them, who would have the first dance, and those things that thrilled debutantes at their first ball, the girls departed.

Slapping her fan in her hand, Sera dropped her smile. Now *she* had the best vantage.

Taking their position framed by the grotto, she flicked her wrist and fanned herself absently as she surveyed the crowd. There was a shocking proliferation of bright colour: reds and blues, oranges and pinks. Lace and ruffles choked gowns, and after years of muslin and cotton, some had ventured into expensive silks. Her own gown lacked embellishment, but that would only make her stand out from the crowd. Should she also change her colour palette? Currently she wore a rather muted shade of blue, designed to bring out the chestnut highlights in her dark brown hair and the blue flecks in her grey eyes, but perhaps she should go bolder. Maybe this year her signature colour *would* be blue, but with shades ranging from robin's egg and periwinkle to royal and navy.

From across the ballroom, a girl stared openly at her.

Sera frowned. Was the girl simple? There were ways to observe without being obvious about it. Tilting her head, she observed the girl from the corner of her eye. Clearly foreign with brown skin and dark hair, she was dressed in the very height of London fashion, the deep yellow of her gown complementing her skin and setting off her dark eyes. That appeared to be the sum total of her intrigue. She stood with no one of note, and she had attracted little notice from anyone who was anyone.

Dismissing her, Sera continued her perusal.

"Lady Seraphina, a delight as always."

How very tiresome. "Your Grace," she said flatly.

The Duke of Sutton offered her what no doubt would be termed a charming smirk, one that said he knew of his attractiveness—with his wealth and his title and his handsomeness—and he also knew one should be flattered he deigned to acknowledge you. "Come, my dear, surely we have a greater acquaintance than that? Last year, you called me Sutton."

"That was last year," she said dismissively.

"Last year, you also permitted...familiarities."

Was he going to be tiresome about everything? "As I said, that was last year."

"What has changed between then and now?" he asked silkily.

"For one, the year."

The slightest of frowns touched his forehead. "Why are you being so difficult?"

Annoyance began to swirl within her. He knew the rules of the game. They had enjoyed a flirtation, one that benefited them both and had always had an expiry. The Duke of Sutton was notorious for his flirtations and the trail of broken hearts he left behind; he was ruthless, unfeeling, and had made many a lady weep. Why was he attempting to prolong what had already died? "I am not difficult, Your Grace. I am bored. There is a difference."

"Bored? Bored? With *me*?"

She exhaled. "I am no longer interested. You may leave."

"You? Are dismissing *me*?"

With a snap of her wrist, she extended her fan and proceeded to ignore him.

"You will regret this," he threatened.

She flicked him a glance. "Will I?"

He smiled tightly and then, finally, he let her be,

disappearing into the crowd.

Ugh, now her stomach was twisted in knots. Why did the duke have to approach her? Her plan for the ball had not included his histrionics, and she hadn't required his petty threats. Fanning herself rhythmically, she breathed in, and then out. In, out. Slowly, the churn in her stomach subsided.

Her gaze locked on two familiar faces amongst the crowd. Lady Elizabeth Harcourt and Miss Maria Spencer froze, their faces draining of colour as they noticed her glare. Quickly, they hurried to her side.

"Lady Seraphina," Elizabeth exclaimed. "You are early!"

"I? *I* am early?"

Elizabeth blanched. "We are late?" she offered.

"I told you both *precisely* when I would be here. Imagine my surprise upon arrival when I discovered not only were you absent, but the position I had chosen specifically for this first ball was occupied by first years."

They glanced at each other. "We apologise," Maria said. "However, you will not mind when we tell you what Margaret Williamson told us—"

"It does not matter what Margaret Williamson told you. I specifically instructed you reserve this grotto and you did not do so."

"But Margaret Williamson told us—"

Sera held up her hand. Maria fell silent. "I do not care what you discovered."

Maria opened her mouth. "But—"

Narrowing her eyes, Sera shot her a look.

"The Marchioness Demartine, Lady Alexandra Torrence, Lady Lydia Torrence," the majordomo intoned.

Sera whipped around. Lips pressed together, she watched as Lady Demartine entered the ballroom flanked by her daughters.

"That's what we were trying to tell you. Lydia Torrence is back." Elizabeth said weakly.

Ignoring Elizabeth, Sera kept her gaze trained on the new arrivals. Lady Demartine was still a beauty, her dark brows a curious contrast with her pale hair. Neither of her daughters had inherited her colouring, with Lady Alexandra's hair a more golden shade of blonde and Sera knew her eyes to be of a muddy sort. Lydia's hair was red, her eyes bright blue-green hazel. Some seemed to think Lydia was beautiful.

Sera gritted her teeth. Fine, Lydia *was* beautiful. Red-gold hair tumbled around her head, her features perfect, with a curvaceous figure just a shade on the right side of ladylike. The gentlemen would flock to her side, but if her affections remained as they had always been, they were doomed to disappointment.

Lady Alexandra was the same age as Sera but had made her debut the year after her. Sera smiled thinly. And what a disaster it had been. Lady Alexandra was…odd. She was fascinated by spirits and cared not who knew it. She was exuberant in everything she did—too bright, too eager, too *much*. It would bear her well if she was just…less.

Sera's gaze slid again to Lydia. Lady Lydia Torrence, recently returned from an extended tour of the Continent. She seemed to have gained polish and poise, and an easy confidence that would draw others to her. That, coupled with her ridiculous beauty, would make her the hit of the Ton. No longer wide-eyed, her thoughts were disguised behind a faintly amused smile. Her smile brightened, however, when her gaze lit upon Lady Violet Crafers. With a quick word to her mother, she crossed the ballroom to join Lady Violet, her smile genuine as she reached her friend's side.

"There is a rumour the Earl of Roxwaithe will be in attendance as well."

"Hmm?" She glanced at Elizabeth.

"Alice Stamford said she heard it from Georgina Parkerson, who heard it from Caroline Bennett, and you know Caroline Bennett knows everything," Elizabeth continued.

"He *never* attends balls," Maria breathed.

"He sometimes attends," Sera said absently. Her mind raced. That would not be why, though. It wasn't a coincidence the earl chose to attend just as Lydia Torrence made her return.

Once, forever ago, she'd been friendly with Lydia Torrence and the girl had taken her in confidence, telling her of her life-long crush on the earl. The earl, though, was fourteen years Lydia's elder and clearly would not be interested in a girl barely seventeen who he no doubt regarded as a much younger sister. Sera, helpfully, had informed Lydia of this and had attempted to turn her from such a fruitless affection. She had, quite helpfully, told others of Lydia's crush, to show the girl how ridiculous it was. Lydia, though, had overreacted to her kind action, screaming and crying and declaring Sera a terrible fiend.

Their friendship had soured after that.

"The earl *is* in attendance," Maria breathed.

"Where?" Sera searched the ballroom.

"There." Maria pointed.

Sure enough, the Earl of Roxwaithe had entered the ballroom. Sera frowned over his appearance. He was so...hairy. Long golden-brown hair was tied back in a knot at the nape of his neck, while his jaw was covered by a beard. He was so...unusual. Few gentlemen of her acquaintance had hair of his length, and none sported a beard

His gaze immediately sought out Lydia Torrence. She had not yet seen him, and he seemed to drink her in. Possibly it was the first time he had seen her since her return, but in any event he displayed his emotion as clearly as if he had shouted.

Some years after the incident with Lydia, it had become apparent Sera had been mistaken in her assessment of the earl. He clearly returned Lydia's affections, and that gave Sera all the ammunition she needed to taunt Lydia—who just as clearly had no clue—at every turn.

She smiled thinly. One did not spurn Lady Seraphina Waller-Mitchell and not live to regret it.

Unaware of Sera's thoughts, Elizabeth asked, "Will you choose a gentleman this year?"

"Don't I always?" Every year it amused her to choose a gentleman to flirt with and beguile. Last year it had been the Duke of Sutton. This year... Her gaze drifted to Lydia Torrence. "Perhaps I will entertain myself with an earl this season."

"An earl?" Maria asked in confusion.

"The Earl of Roxwaithe, Maria. Honestly." Sometimes she questioned why she associated with them.

Elizabeth frowned. "But he is never in society, Sera. There is no point."

"He will attend enough this season," she said dismissively.

"How do you know?"

Lydia Torrence was here and it followed the Earl of Roxwaithe would be where she is. "It is a feeling. Do not distract me." She levelled her gaze on the earl.

Still he watched Lydia Torrence. They both couldn't be more obvious if they tried. It would be pointless to attempt to attract his attention. While she enjoyed a challenge, she did not enjoy failure and that way lay nothing but frustration. However, if she remembered correctly, the earl had a brother. "What is the name of the younger brother to the Earl of Roxwaithe?"

Maria blinked. "The one who is dead?" she asked hesitantly.

"No." She remembered his name, of course. Everyone remembered that tragedy. Lord Maxim Farlisle, the youngest of the brothers, lost at sea these eight years past. What he had been doing on a ship to the Americas to begin with had caused furious speculation amongst the Ton at the time, though none could determine exactly why he had sought that passage. "The one who is alive."

Elizabeth and Maria exchanged glances and then gave her blank looks.

Impatience made her tone harsh. "Well?"

"I do not know, Seraphina," Elizabeth said hastily.

"He plays football on a heath outside the city," Maria offered.

Sera's brows shot up. "The brother of an earl? Playing football? In *public*? How do you know this?"

Maria blanched. "I—I don't know. I just do."

"But you do not know his name?"

"Stephen!" Triumph lit Maria's expression. "It is Stephen!"

Lord Stephen Farlisle. "Is he in attendance this evening?"

Maria opened her mouth but uttered no sound. Elizabeth bit her lip.

Honestly, did she have to do everything herself? "Lady Asterd knows everyone and everything. Go find her."

They scurried to do her bidding. Sera returned her contemplation to the earl pretending he did not watch Lady Lydia while she pretended she took no notice of him at all.

In short order, Maria returned, breathless. "Lady Asterd said he attends this evening. He is in the ballroom."

Sera immediately turned her gaze to the throng. "Where?"

Maria searched. "There," she said, pointing.

On the opposite side of the ballroom, a lone gentleman stood, seemingly disinclined to change that state. He was unimpressive, for all he was tall, and though his shoulders were broad he was far too slender for her liking. His clothing was sombre and did not mould to his form, and his unsmiling face was not handsome: his brow too high, his nose too bold, his jaw too strong. His mouth, however, was full and sensual, his lips plush and sulky and the only softness in that harsh face. Blond hair did not riot in a tumble of curls as other gentlemen's did, the short, straight strands pomaded close to his skull. She could not determine his eye colour from this distance, but she would wager a guinea it was some shade of brown. What shade she would determine that upon engineering their acquaintance.

She frowned. From the depths of her memory, she recalled him from her first—or was it her second?—season. He had been merry and dashing and wicked, and he and his friends had delighted in thumbing their noses at the strictures of society. His clothing had been the pip of fashion, his hair the careless tumble of curls one could only achieve with hours of styling. Then he had disappeared for some time, and talk of scandal had emerged, something about carriages and duels and maybe even a death? The gossip had died down, as it always did, and she had promptly forgotten about him.

Until now. Now, he served a purpose. Now, he would facilitate her irritating Lydia Torrence.

Dismissing those barely recalled memories, she focused instead on the present. No doubt she would discover more as their acquaintance progressed and, if it was relevant, she would address it then.

"Where did you find Lady Asterd?" she asked.

"With the other matrons in the retiring room. Why?"

"I require an introduction and, as I said, Lady Asterd knows everyone."

Maria frowned. "But Sera, Lady Asterd does not like you."

"I know." Affecting a dazzling smile, she asked, "I am put together?"

Still frowning, Maria replied, "Of course."

"Make sure we retain the grotto," Sera instructed and then she swept away to find Lady Asterd.

She had a man to beguile.

Chapter Two

LORD STEPHEN FARLISLE WAS doing his level best to avoid the Earl of Roxwaithe. It wasn't too hard a feat. His brother didn't seem inclined to associate with him either.

Exhaling, he cast his gaze around the ballroom. Usually, he avoided balls and assemblies like the plague, but the coffers of the foundation were never deep enough and a ball might mean members of the Ton were more inclined to reach into their pockets. If he could get them to throw some guineas his way, he could endure an hour or two.

Raising his hand, he stifled a yawn. He'd been up since half five that morning and, as the clocks now rapidly approached midnight, he was battling to stay awake. Knowing he was to attend the ball this evening, he should have forced himself to remain in bed, but he found it hard to sleep in, his body now well used to rising with the sun. Every morning, at a little past sunrise, he made his way out to the heath. Few milled about at that hour, and thus there were none to see as he performed the morning exercises that had become his routine. He didn't mind the stretching and running, but the shock of the water as he swam in the heath's freezing lake was uniformly bracing. The lifting of weights, though, he truly despised. These past four days, he'd neglected the exercise and he was paying for it now. If it weren't for the fact his body would seize even more, and it would be that much harder to get himself back to half as good, he would be thankful to never again perform such a vile exercise.

Subtly, he rotated his shoulders. They were aching a little, old injuries making themselves known. He'd dislocated his shoulder six months ago on the pitch, and though it had mostly healed, it troubled him at odd moments. However, it was merely one ache amongst many, and newer than the rest. He'd had these last seven years or more to get used to a body that didn't always work as it should, and lingering aches and pains that reminded him of past recklessness and stupidity.

Across from him, Lord Gray entered the ballroom. Finally, one of the reasons Stephen had attended had arrived. Lord Gray had more wealth than he knew what to do with and the rumour was he would gift to anyone with a half-decent story.

Setting his step toward Lord Gray, he recited yet again his appeal in his head. He'd practiced all of yesterday and today, with variations depending on whom he would be pitching it to. "Lord Gray," he greeted.

His lordship turned. "Yes?"

"Lord Stephen Farlisle, my lord."

His brow creased. "Who?"

Christ. "Roxwaithe's brother," he reluctantly clarified.

Recognition lit Lord Gray's expression. Of course it bloody did. Everyone knew his bloody brother. "Ah, Roxwaithe. Good man. And you're his brother?"

Stephen held on to his pleasant expression. "Yes."

"Good. Good. Damned crush, this. Can't put two thoughts together."

Pushing aside his ire, Stephen continued, "I wonder if I might bend your ear on an investment opportunity."

"What? Loud as the dickens in here."

Stephen raised his voice. "An investment opportunity, but also a charitable one."

"What? Charity? Don't know much about that. Have to ask Lady Gray on that one. She's the one who likes doffing out coin on unfortunates."

"This is both, Gray."

"An investment, you say?" Gray looked him over. "Discussed this investment with your brother?"

Stephen gritted his teeth. "Of course." In that he'd mentioned his intention to form a foundation to his brother once in passing and Oliver had grunted in return.

"Always gets in on the ground floor, Roxwaithe. Doubled his fortune, rumour has it."

"My brother is astute." And miserly, and judgemental, and an all around arse.

"Yes, well, better at managing dosh, isn't he? *Doubled* his fortune." He nodded sagely.

Stephen's hands curled to fists. Lord Gray didn't mean that as a dig. The man clearly didn't know anything about Stephen's own fortune, or to be precise, his lack of one. "Shall I attend you tomorrow, Gray?"

"If you want. Will make sure her ladyship is also present. She's the one who likes charities, what." Lord Gray's gaze drifted past him.

Stephen knew when to retreat. "Thank you, Gray," he said and, with a stiff bow, he left.

As he circled the ballroom, he consulted his pocket watch. Twenty more minutes and it would not be untoward of him to leave. With one opportunity gained, the ball wasn't a complete waste.

Absently, he rotated his wrist, the action not entirely fluid. Once, he'd lived for amusement, the wilder the better. Who would have thought at the age of almost thirty-one he would be desirous most of his bed? And what's more, to be alone in it.

From across the ballroom, a woman stared.

He stared back. A small smile played about her rosebud mouth as she noticed his regard. Dark hair piled atop her head, a few tendrils teasing a long, creamy neck that flowed into straight shoulders and an impressive bosom.

Stephen kept his expression impassive. Her name sat on the tip of his tongue and he was certain he would have been introduced to her at one point or another. However, his first season had been spent in pursuit of reckless decadence, and the second he'd hied to the Continent with Harbor. His third and fourth... He'd been unable to do much of anything in what would have been his third and fourth.

Flicking her fan open, her gaze met his over the top of it, one delicate brow arching.

His own brows drew into a frown. Was she flirting with him?

"Lord Stephen," a soft voice beside him said.

He stiffened. Ah, bollocks. "Good evening, my lady."

Lady Demartine's expression was faintly chiding. "It has been an age since I have seen you, Lord Stephen," she gently rebuked.

"I have been...busy," he said lamely.

"Too busy to even enjoy a cup of tea?"

He opened his mouth to say again he'd been busy but that chiding expression halted him. Lady Demartine was as a mother to him, and as his had died when he was a child, she was the only mother he knew. He *hated* disappointing her.

"I have missed you, Stephen," she said. "Demartine and I both."

"Yes, my lady."

She looped her arm through his. "Take a turn with me and tell me what you have been up to."

"Nothing," he said as they began their tour.

"Ah, you men," she said, a smile in her voice. "All of you are the same. You say you never do anything and then, five minutes later, one cannot stop your talk of everything and anything. How is your football team?"

"They—we—go well."

"And the children you teach?"

"Coach, Lady Demartine. It is called coaching."

"Ah. The children you coach, how are they?"

"Also well."

Her mouth kicked up. "Perhaps I was wrong, Stephen. Perhaps you do not speak of everything and anything."

He ducked his head again, this time to conceal a smile. "How are you, my lady?"

"Ah, changing the subject. Well played, Stephen," she teased.

Though his cheeks heated, his grin widened. Lady Demartine always saw straight through him.

"When was the last time you saw your brother?"

His smile died abruptly. "I don't know."

She shook her head. "You two. You would think with everything that has occurred you would be closer."

"He started it," he said sullenly, and then cursed himself for the childish remark.

Lady Demartine's knowing gaze weighted heavy upon him. "I daresay you are both old enough to handle your relationship yourselves, even if you do not act like it." She sighed. "At least we see you at a ball. Perhaps treat your brother kindly, though. There is much to which he has had to adjust."

His hands clenched into fists. "And he? Should he treat me kindly?"

Surprised lit her expression. "He does, Stephen."

He shrugged.

Shaking her head, she said again, "You two."

Clenching his jaw, he took a breath. Lady Demartine meant well, he knew. "I beg your pardon, madam, but I find myself in need of refreshment."

She gazed at him levelly. "Do you?" she finally said.

His neck heated again. How did she always know when he was prevaricating?

She shook her head. "No matter. Go, Stephen. I shan't keep you when you don't want to converse."

Bowing sharply, he departed, pretending he couldn't feel her gaze between his shoulder blades as he left. The refreshment room held nothing stronger than an orgeat lemonade, and he grimaced as he drank. He'd never liked the flavour, and it was especially bad when watered down in this manner. Handing his cup to a footman, he blanched as he was accosted by a whirl of ruffles and lace.

"Lord Stephen!" Lady Asterd cried.

He winced. "Lady Asterd."

A matronly woman loosely acquainted with Lady Demartine, Lady Asterd had in seasons past introduced him to numerous eligible debutantes in an attempt to match-make. She had been decidedly unsuccessful.

"Thank goodness I found you before that vile girl did," she exclaimed.

His brows shot up. Lady Asterd was not known for her subtlety, but even that was a bit much.

"I would never forgive myself if I allowed you to fall in her clutches. It would cause my dear friend such distress, and Lady Demartine has had too many tragedies in her life. Why, there was poor, lost Maxim, of course." Producing a handkerchief from her gown, she held it to her eye.

"Of course." Because the death of his younger brother eleven years ago did not affect him, Stephen, in any way at all.

"And your dear mother. Such friends we were, though I was a little older than them. Bosom companions, always together at each ball. They even married within months of each other and then, for your poor mother to pass bringing your poor brother into the world, and then he departing not a dozen years later—"

"Maxim was fifteen," he interrupted.

Her ladyship blinked. "Pardon?"

Lady Asterd had no notion what she said could be upsetting to him, and he couldn't be bothered explaining it to her. "Nothing, Lady Asterd. You were saying something about a girl?"

"Yes! Lady Seraphina Waller-Mitchell! Do not fall for her wicked wiles, Lord Stephen."

Never, in all his life, had he fallen prey to a woman's wiles. When he was younger, he knew the game and he played it well. Now...it all seems so false, and he had no time for falsity. Except when it came to his brother. He would prevaricate and obfuscate until the cows came home for Oliver. "I shall be sure not to do so, my lady."

"Good. Good. She is a wicked sort, that one."

A spark of interest flared; Lady Asterd's vehemence almost made him want to seek the woman out to see what was so very wicked about her. Almost. "Thank you, I shall take your words under advisement."

She nodded importantly. "Good. Good. I could not bear it if something happened and I did not warn you."

"Of course," he said ironically.

Her gaze flitted past him. "Oh, I must—Lady Walpole! My apologies, Lord Stephen, but— Lady Walpole!"

Rolling his shoulders, he watched as she rushed away to accost Lady Walpole. Thank Christ that was over. Lady Asterd was tolerable in small doses—very small doses.

From across the ballroom, the woman smiled at him archly. Lady Seraphina Waller-Mitchell. Wickedness personified, apparently.

Behind her, staring at Lydia Torrence like the obvious clodpole he was, stood Oliver. Christ, he had no desire to be forced to converse with his brother. Turning on his heel, Stephen departed the ballroom.

The balcony was fairly deserted for such a crowded ball. A few gentlemen smoked, and some ladies gathered to take in the night air. Stephen found a deserted corner and leant against the balustrade, inhaling evening blossoms, perfume, and cheroot smoke. A hint of rain threaded the air, speaking of summer storms.

He rubbed a hand across his face. He didn't know if he had it in him to take another pass around the ballroom. He was not used to society and, it was plain, society was not used to him.

Someone stumbled into him, a whirl of pale blue. Automatically he caught her, dark hair bobbing at his chin as she gripped his forearms.

"Thank you, my lord," she said breathily. Still gripping him, she looked up.

He drew in a breath. It was the woman from the ballroom. The wicked one.

Tilted grey eyes framed with thick dark lashes stared up at him from a heart-shaped face. A pale blue gown clothed her, the square neckline framing truly magnificent breasts...though he questioned how much was her and how much clever undergarments. Interestingly, though, she was no more than a head shorter than him, and he was accounted a tall man

Expression coy, she gazed at him through her lashes. "However can I thank you, sir? You have saved me from a dire fate."

"A slight stumble is a dire fate?"

Her brow creased slightly before clearing, a dazzling smile taking its place. "What could be worse than a lady tearing her hem?"

"What indeed," he murmured. Clearly, she had performed this apparent artlessness a hundred times and, just as clearly, it usually worked. It was...affecting, he granted her. Play the damsel in distress and position him as the triumphant hero. If he'd had a different frame of mind, it might have even worked. As it was, he saw straight through her ploy. Why she'd chosen him out of all the gentlemen he couldn't say.

Her smile slipped somewhat as he declined to comment further. "But as I said, I must thank you."

"There is no need."

"Surely there is some way I can show my gratitude?" Her smile was an alluring mix of innocence and archness. Lady Asterd had been right. This woman and wickedness were well-acquainted.

His own wickedness prompted him. "Do you often find this works?" he asked conversationally.

Her smile froze. "I beg your pardon?"

"The helpless damsel seeking the assistance of a big, brave, strong gentleman. What is next? Will you insinuate the promise of a kiss only to deny it? We are, after all, in full view of the ballroom."

She drew in a sharp breath, her grey eyes wide.

"You play this game well, I admit," he continued. "I would even warrant most would not even know they were playing counterpart. It is admirable."

Scowling, she set herself from him and pulled herself straight. She forgot to position herself to best advantage, her cheeks pinkening as she struggled to contain her ire. He watched, fascinated. This woman was vastly more interesting.

"*You*," she spat, "are not acting as you ought."

"Oh? And how ought I act?"

"With respect. With dignity. With *gentlemanly* concern."

Enjoying himself immensely, he twisted the knife. "I was unaware this was my role."

"You should be flattered by my attention. Flattered! Do you know who I am? What my condescension means?"

"Clearly, I do not."

"I am sought after. I am the one everyone wishes to know. My favour has the ability to make or break a season."

He shrugged.

She looked as if she would explode. "You are no gentleman."

"I never claimed otherwise."

"You are so vexing!"

"I did not think I could inspire such passion on so short an acquaintance."

"And yet, you have," she replied snidely.

"Perhaps, then, you should focus your attention on another more worthy."

Abruptly, her passion faded and her eyes narrowed. "Should I?"

Unease skittered through him. Somehow, he had lost control…but then, what did he care? He had left this game long ago and he had no desire to return. She was interesting, he granted, and perhaps if he was as he had been, he would have enjoyed sparring with her. But he wasn't as he had been. Too much had happened for him to ever be that foolish and selfish again. "I find I have had enough of the air. I bid you good evening." Bowing sharply, he made for the French doors.

"You are leaving?" she said, disbelief threading her tone.

"As I said."

"You can't just *leave*. You are not—"

He didn't hear the end of her sentence, the din of chatter and laugher as he entered the ball drowning out her words. He was at this ball for one reason: to raise funds. She had made him forget, and that he could not allow.

Setting his shoulders, he made for the richest pockets he could pick.

Chapter Three

"HIGGINS!" SERA STORMED THROUGH the entrance hall of Tidswell House. Why were servants never around when one needed them? "Higgins!"

As if by magic, her butler materialised. "I'm here, my lady. What did you require?"

"Where is the blackboard, Higgins? It was supposed to be in the Blue Room an hour ago."

"I believe Johnson is bringing it now, my lady."

"An hour ago, Higgins. It was supposed to be there an hour ago!"

"We had trouble removing it from the nursery," Higgins said calmly. "It will be in place when Miss Maria and Lady Elizabeth arrive."

Throwing her hands in the air, Sera stomped into the blue room and flopped onto the chaise. Her foot immediately started to tap.

Higgins followed her. "It will be in place, my lady," he repeated.

Crossing her arms, she tried to still her tapping foot. "It had better be, Higgins, or I shall let you off without reference."

"Yes, my lady."

"Everything must be perfect." Her foot wouldn't still.

"I know, Lady Seraphina," he said gently.

Everything had to be perfect. Everything. Teeth worrying her bottom lip, she again attempted to force her foot still. This time, she managed it.

Opening eyes she hadn't realised she'd closed, she met Higgins warm, gentle gaze. "Without a reference, Higgins," she said without sting.

The faints of smiles touched his lips. "Of course."

She toyed with a fold in her dress. "Did a letter come from my father?"

A pause and then, "No, my lady."

The silk was cool against her fingers. Her father sent a letter at the beginning of each quarter. That he was a week or so late was not unusual. He was a busy man. Perhaps it had slipped his mind. It had happened before. "Perhaps it will come next week."

"Perhaps."

Lifting her gaze, she said, "Thank you, Higgins."

Compassion filled Higgins's eyes. "Yes, my lady." Bowing, he closed the door behind him.

Taking a steadying breath, she leant her head back on the chaise. Maria and Elizabeth would be here soon and she needed to gather herself before they arrived. She focussed on the frieze surrounding the chandelier. Leaves twined around florets in the centre circle and accented the corners of the surrounding square. Swirls and dips created a maze along the square's thick border, one she'd solved a thousand times with her gaze.

Last night had not happened as it should, but then, Lord Stephen Farlisle had not acted as a gentleman ought. He'd ignored every single one of her overtures, and so she'd broken her own rule and pursued him on to the balcony. Usually, gentlemen came to her and, if they ignored her, she would choose another. However, another would not annoy Lydia Torrence.

She pictured him as he'd been last night. The light spilling from the ballroom had slashed harshness into already severe features, dark eyes shadowing heavy brows while cutting a sharp jaw and even sharper cheekbones. Blond hair darkened by pomade and slicked against his skull only added to the severity.

He had been taller than her, which in itself was unusual. She usually stood of a height with most men, but Lord Stephen was at least a head taller. Up close, the build she had thought thin had instead been revealed as lean, his coat outlining broad shoulders, though it hung a loose around his waist and hips. His breeches had also been loose at his thighs and waist though his stockings displayed well-turned calves. He was not altogether unattractive, but he was certainly not as handsome as the men she usually chose to associate with.

She had watched him in the ballroom, and not one lady approached him, just as he had no smile for any lady present. He had conversed with Lords Gray and Boakan, and had lingered near the Duke of Meacham, but it seemed dancing and flirtation had not been on his card. He should have been flattered at the attention of a lady, especially one as sought after as she.

And yet, he had not acted as he ought.

Perhaps she had become complacent. Usually, a pretty smile and a well-timed compliment drew most to her side. Lord Stephen, however, had seen right through her artifice, had laughed and taunted her. For a moment, he had been as wicked as Lady Asterd thought she, Sera, to be. But then, the wickedness had bled from him and his sharp features had become severe once more. And then, unforgivably, he had abandoned her.

She had gaped after him, unable to believe he had literally turned on his heel and *abandoned* her. Around her, people had tittered and whispered, their expressions gleeful. Lifting her chin, she'd arranged a pretty smile on her face and swept from the balcony, as if Lord Stephen acting the boor had always been her plan. She maintained her smile and her air as she had collected Maria and Elizabeth—people who acted as they *ought*—and headed for the retiring room. As soon as she'd found them a secluded spot, she'd let her pretty smile drop. "Lord Stephen Farlisle. What have you discovered?"

Maria and Elizabeth had exchanged a look. "We were to discover things?" Maria asked cautiously.

Sera scowled. "What were you even *doing*?"

"I was talking with Margaret Mayhew about Venice," Elizabeth offered.

"And Lord Palmer asked me to dance," Maria said.

Ugh. Useless, the both of them. "We are to convene tomorrow at Tidswell House," she announced. "We must learn everything there is to know about Lord Stephen Farlisle."

They exchanged another look. "How are we to do that?" Elizabeth asked.

"I don't know, however you usually do it," she said caustically "Tomorrow. Tidswell House. Eleven o'clock."

And now it was tomorrow at—Sera glanced at the clock on the mantle—a quarter to eleven. For whatever else they were, Elizabeth and Maria were punctual.

They were also excellent information-gathers, and would no doubt have a wealth of knowledge on Lord Stephen. She herself did not know much about him, apart from he was a rude boor, and what little she did would most likely fit in a small corner of the blackboard that would *eventually* reach the blue room: He was the younger brother of the Earl of Roxwaithe; his family was close with Lydia Torrence's family; and his younger brother had died years ago.

She frowned. She should know more. It did not matter he did not often frequent balls and assemblies of the Ton—she should know everything about everyone.

"Lady Elizabeth Harcourt and Miss Maria Spencer," Higgins announced.

Jerking herself to proper posture, she smoothed her hair as Higgins admitted Elizabeth and Maria to the blue room. "Thank you, Higgins. And the blackboard?"

"Johnson has been momentarily delayed," the butler replied.

She exhaled impatiently. "I suppose in the meantime we shall have tea. Let Mrs Broadbent know."

"Yes, my lady." Bowing, he departed.

Elizabeth and Maria had settled on the chaise opposite her. Elizabeth arranging her skirts about her while Maria looked at Sera expectantly, her hands clasped in her lap.

"Well?" Sera said. "What have you discovered?"

"Lord Stephen Farlisle is the younger brother of the Earl of Roxwaithe," Maria announced.

Sera rolled her eyes. "Everyone knows that."

"Do they also know they are estranged?" Maria did not wait for a reaction to that before she continued. "They hide it well, ably assisted by Lord Stephen's frequent absence from society, but my information is they have not spent above ten minutes together for the better part of a year."

Sera sat back on the chaise. Well, that was a surprise. The earl and his brother did indeed hide it well, though now she thought on it, she could not recall they spoke once at the ball the previous evening. In fact, with this information at hand, it was now clear they actively sought to avoid each other. How very interesting.

"I heard he ran through his inheritance from his mother before he was three and twenty," Elizabeth added. "And he disappeared for four years. There are all sorts of rumours about that time. Some even say he killed a man."

Sera scoffed. "That's outlandish."

"It is, isn't it? And yet, many seem to believe it."

"Who on earth do they think he killed?"

"Lord Harbor. You remember him: He was fabulously wealthy. His family was taken by a fever when he was two and he inherited *everything*. Anyway, he and Lord Stephen were great friends until they both disappeared. Then word came Lord Harbor had died in a carriage accident, and the rumour was Lord Stephen engineered it. Lord Harbor had no heirs and very little of his fortune was entailed, so it was bequeathed as per the terms of his will."

"And Lord Stephen supposedly murdered him over this?" It sounded all stuff and nonsense to her.

Elizabeth nodded. "Apparently it didn't help he was much changed upon his return. He was a wicked scamp upon his debut to society, he and Lord Harbor and their friends pulling prank after prank, indiscriminate flirting, wild wagers and foolishness."

"So, a typical young gentleman."

A smile lifted Elizabeth's lips. "Yes. When he returned, though, he was sober as a cleric, and he fairly disappeared from society. The rumours died down—"

"Mostly," Maria interjected.

"Mostly." Elizabeth amended.

Sera frowned. "Why do I not remember this?" She took pride in knowing everything. *Everything*. This was salacious enough she should have long since become an expert.

Maria cleared her throat. "The rumours first started when you were in Paris those five months."

Oh. Sera averted her gaze. Paris. When she'd gone to meet her father and he...had not come. She shook herself. "But after that?"

Elizabeth lifted a shoulder. "Perhaps we simply weren't interested?"

"Perhaps." She vaguely recalled something that could have been these rumours, but possibly it was as Elizabeth said— she simply had not been interested enough to care.

A slight scratch at the door signalled the arrival of the tea service. They fell silent as Millie and Veronica arranged the tea and sweets. "Are these the shortbreads, Veronica?" Sera asked.

The maid paused. "No, milady. I don't believe Mrs

Travers baked any this morning. Would you like her to?"

"No, no." She looked over the treats on display, her gaze catching on one in particular. "Gingernuts?"

"Yes, milady," Veronica confirmed warily.

"Excellent. I do enjoy Mrs Travers's gingernuts. You may go."

Veronica bobbed a curtsey, as did Millie. "Thank you, milady," they said.

After they had departed, Sera picked up the teapot. "What else have you discovered, perhaps something a little more concrete than rumoured murders?"

"He has no discernible wealth, and has taken bachelor's rooms in a modest residence in Belgravia," Elizabeth said while Maria eyed off the gingernuts. "He does not seem interested in increasing his fortune through the taking of a bride."

Pouring the tea, Sera snorted. "Half the Ton has no discernible wealth; no doubt his brother finances him. And if he has no interest in wealth, then why would he shackle himself with a wife? What about lately?"

"Lately?" Maria asked around a mouthful of gingernuts

"Yes. This is all of his life in the past. What of his life now?"

Maria swallowed. "Mrs Travers does make good gingernuts."

"She does. Lord Stephen?"

Maria exchanged a look with Elizabeth. "My brother often sees him exercising?" she offered. "Richard often takes early morning walks, and he has mentioned he has seen Lord Stephen undertaking exercise." Maria lowered her voice. "Apparently, he swims."

Good god, she'd heard it all now. What member of quality swam? In *London*?

"And Richard says he plays football. That's how I knew, last night at the ball. He plays it with the lower classes," Maria added.

Sera's brows shot up. Who *was* this man? He did *nothing* as he ought. "He is contrary, is he not?"

Shrugging, Maria pilfered another gingernut and shoved it in her mouth.

"My brother sees him often at a gaming hell." Lifting her tea cup, Elizabeth took a sip.

"Don't all gentlemen?" Sipping her own tea, Sera sighed.

"Which one?"

"The 1810 Club. My brother says it's the most amusing establishment. He says there are cards, and gaming, and there are even four billiards tables, and the quality of the liquor is second to none. Best whisky he's ever tasted, apparently. Lord Stephen owns part of it with several other gentlemen. It was bequeathed by Lord Harbor."

"I suppose this club is why he murdered Lord Harbor," Sera remarked sardonically.

Elizabeth grinned. "Perhaps indeed. My brother has offered to smuggle me in a time or two. I am tempted to agree."

Shaking her head, Sera said, "Your brother is an anarchist."

Elizabeth's grin widened. "I know." Her smile faded. "What do you seek with him?"

"Pardon?"

"Lord Stephen. What is it you seek from him?"

Maria paused in her annihilation of the gingernuts, her gaze darting between Elizabeth and Sera.

She sat back. She...had no idea. She'd had the vague notion of toying with him, watching gleefully as Lydia Torrence spluttered impotently, but now...well, now Lord Stephen himself intrigued her. She had no notion of what she sought, but perhaps that would be part of the fun. "I am not certain. At this stage, let us gather information and see what we can see."

Outside the door, a loud clatter sounded. Jerking her head, she watched as Johnson arm-wrestled the blackboard through the door. "Excuse me, my lady. Apologies for the noise, and the lateness. Was a right struggle getting this here blackboard down from the nursery. Where would you like it?"

"By the mantle, Johnson."

Nodding, he shoved and stumbled the blackboard into position and, with another nod, left them. "Maria, do record all we have learnt about Lord Stephen," Sera said.

Ridding her hands of crumbs, Maria stood and started scribbling on the blackboard. Once all the information had been recorded, Sera stared at it while Elizabeth took a sip of tea and Maria dusted chalk from her hands. Lord Stephen made no sense. There was little reason to suppose their paths would cross in a seemingly natural manner at any point in the near future. She would, it seemed, have to seek him out. But where? How?

It seemed they would have to think on this further.

"Settle in, ladies," she said. "We still have much to do."

Chapter Four

MAKING HIS WAY AROUND the side of his family's London townhouse, Stephen entered Roxegate through the servant's access. The door opened to the kitchen, where the family cook stood at the wooden bench with her back to him, rolling some sort of dough. "Mrs Parsons, how are you?"

"Lord above!" Whirling around, Mrs Parsons's hand flew to her chest, leaving a floury imprint upon her dress. "Lord Stephen, what are you doing, coming in this way?" she scolded.

"I wanted to see you," he said, eyeing the pastries set to cool on metal racks. They looked to be lemon tarts, his favourite.

"Well, you should be coming through the front door, as befits a man of your station." She pointed her rolling pin at him. "I suppose you'll be wanting a pastry."

"You suppose right."

"Well then, take one. I don't have all day to entertain you."

Pilfering a pastry from the smart row, he took a bite. Flaky, buttery, with the sharp tang of lemon. Delicious.

"I suppose also you'll be wanting to see your brother," Mrs Parsons said as she returned to rolling dough.

The pastry abruptly tasted like ash on his tongue. "Again, you suppose right," he said, lowering the pastry.

"Don't be vexing him. He's had a hard day—a hard *week*—the poor love."

Stephen made a non-committal sound. As if his brother had ever had a hard day in his life.

From the side of her eye, Mrs Parsons looked at him. "Now, don't be like that. I know you and he have your troubles, but he tries his best and the week has not been kind. You know Lady Lydia has returned."

"I know."

"That girl's been gone over a year, and he's been missing her something fierce. He's been on edge ever since she set foot on English soil again."

"I *know*, Mrs Parsons."

"Well, see that you do. He's got the weight of Roxegate on his shoulders, along with all of us, and he has his struggles with Lady Lydia. You mind yourself with him."

"He should just marry her and get it over with," Stephen muttered.

"I've no doubt one day he will, but he isn't there yet. We don't all wake up at the same time. I'm including you, I'll have you know," she said pointedly.

Stephen ducked his head. What was it with the women in his life wanting him to cut Oliver some slack? First Lady Torrence and now Mrs Parsons.

"Take another pastry, and then you can take that tray when you go to see your brother. He hasn't had any lunch."

Stephen eyed the tray to which she pointed, piled with sandwiches, pastries, and fruit. "Aren't there servants for that type of thing?"

"There are."

"I am a lord, I'll have you know. And your employer. I don't undertake menial tasks."

She raised her brows. "You're not my employer."

"Fine. My family employs you."

"Ah, so you do understand his lordship is your brother."

Muscle ticking in his jaw, he glanced askance.

The rhythmic sound of the rolling pin filled the kitchen. "How's your shoulder?" Mrs Parson finally asked.

Stephen exhaled. "Fine."

"You haven't hurt yourself again playing football?"

His lips twitched. Mrs Parsons fussed overmuch. "No."

"And I suppose your team has won another game. Again."

"Well, that's what happens when you're the best."

She snorted. "The best of a bad bunch, I've no doubt."

He grinned. "You know you love us."

"I do. God help me, I do."

"When will we see you again on the heath?"

"I don't know, lad. I can't just run off and watch football matches, I have a job to do."

"So...Saturday, then?'

"Lord, go away with you."

Still grinning, he shoved himself upright. "Right, I'm off," he said, starting for the servant stairs.

"Take the tray with you," Mrs Parsons chided.

Swerving, he took the tray.

"And remember to mind your brother," she called after him as he ascended the stairs.

The tray got heavier with each step he took. His brother's study had once been their father's, and unwanted memories rushed through him. As a child, he'd used to dread the journey to his father's study, each step taking him closer to his father's disdain and disappointment. Unsmiling, his father had always had the same refrain: why can't you be more like your brother? Why can't you be responsible like him? Why can't you be sober like him? Why can't you be productive like him? Why and why and why.

Halting mid-step, Stephen closed his eyes. His father was long dead; it was Oliver's study now. Perfect Oliver, who never displayed more emotion than he should, who excelled at math and science and Latin, who pursued proper gentleman pursuits and was the envy of his peers.

Oliver, the Earl of Roxwaithe and custodian of its riches, who kept the purse-strings strangled shut.

Exhaling, Stephen started again toward the study. Determination filled him, and he pushed any apprehension aside. He was applying to his brother for funds...and he was going to lie about its purpose.

He could never apply directly. Oliver was convinced Stephen was still the spendthrift, careless, miscreant fribble he had been before the accident. It didn't matter how many times he attempted to prove otherwise—Oliver only ever remembered the failures and none of the successes. He had not had to apply to his brother for a good six months, his own investments with what funds he'd managed to raise from Quality he'd approached paying for the establishment and maintenance of the Young Person's Football Charitable Endeavour. However, they were now looking to expand and the fastest way would be to source funds from his brother...who forced him to a merry dance for each ha'penny he bestowed.

And so, he would pretend to be the fribble Oliver thought him and, in the end, he would receive the funds. All it cost was the respect of his brother...but then, he'd never really had Oliver's respect.

The quiet snick of the study door preceded his entry. Placing the tray of sandwiches on a side table, Stephen approached his brother. Oliver sat at his desk, the heel of his hand pressing into his forehead as he continued to work on the report before him. A long strand of blondish-brown hair fell from the queue at the back of his neck, brushing against the unfashionable beard his brother wore. If their father—who despised any man who was not clean-shaven and sported anything other than ruthlessly short hair—could see his eldest son now, he wouldn't think Oliver so bloody perfect.

"What is it, Rajitha?" Oliver asked.

"Your secretary is still in his office," Stephen said

Oliver's head jerked up, surprise colouring his features.

Stephen lowered himself into the seat opposite, keeping his expression carefully blank.

"What brings you to Roxegate, brother?" Oliver finally said.

Right. Let the game begin. "I am here to beg for funds."

Oliver frowned. "You do not have to beg for funds."

No, of course not. That was why he had to come into this study with all its memories and play this game once again. "I should like funds to allow for the continued study of the mythic," he lied.

Oliver blinked. "I beg your pardon?"

"The mythic. The spiritual. That is what Alexandra Torrence calls it, isn't it? You know. Ghosts and such." He'd hit upon this reasoning when he'd seen Alexandra at the ball the previous evening. It was an outlandish enough reason to distract his brother and, when Stephen gave the real reason, his brother was more likely to agree. He had every confidence it would work. He had, after all, done it a hundred times before.

Thoughts of the ball sparked a memory of the woman who'd cornered him on the balcony, of her grey cat's eyes and dark hair and how she'd spat fire when he'd seen through her game. A smirk tugged at him but he struggled to control it. Now was not the time to remember her.

"The spiritual," Oliver said slowly. "You wish to study the spiritual?"

"As I said."

"Since when?"

"Since when what?" he said, just to be annoying.

Oliver gritted his teeth. "When did this interest begin?"

"I have always possessed an interest." It wasn't quite a lie. Vaguely, in the back of his mind, he'd always wondered what Alexandra Torrence found so fascinating about the spiritual.

"Not that I have observed. You were more likely to be outside occupying yourself with some sort of ball sport than traipsing through halls with Alexandra and Maxim hunting ghosts."

He raised a brow. "And if Lord Roxwaithe didn't see it, then it must not have happened?"

"No, I—" Oliver exhaled. "I did not mean it such. It is a surprise. What do you require the funds for?"

"For my studies."

"Yes, I understand, but what specifically? Is there equipment that must be purchased? Dues to be paid? Are you looking for further study? Where, exactly, does one study the spiritual?" He frowned. "I do not recall Lord Demartine mentioning Alexandra petitioning him to fund her interest."

Affecting a scowl, Stephen averted his gaze. "I should have known you would not help."

"I did not say that. It is good practice to ask these questions," Oliver said shortly.

"It is because I come to you with the study of the spiritual, isn't it? If it were an investment or a charity, you would have no concern." He held his breath.

"That is not true, Stephen. You—"

His brother had not noticed the seed. "These funds are mine. They have been invested on my behalf. I am entitled to them."

Oliver exhaled. "I am the trustee and I would be remiss in my duty if I did not question what you will do with these funds. You have announced this interest out of the blue and you give no basis for the release of funds. You have not given any evidence you have done even a cursory exam."

"You are being unreasonable."

"It is unfortunate, then, that you must seek the permission of an unreasonable man," his brother barked. "Demonstrate when you first displayed this interest."

"As I've said. Always. I cannot remember when it began."

"Then what am I to think, brother? Or is this like the time you wanted to run Excott Manor?"

Stephen looked to the side, a muscle ticking in his jaw. Excott Manor had been turned into a facility for the rehabilitation of injured persons, but as the treatments Dr. Griffiths employed were radical and controversial, the facility was run under the guise of a ramshackle country manor. Stephen knew the treatments to be successful. Dr. Griffiths had, after all, treated him, when he was broken and ruined and convinced he would never walk again. After his recovery, he'd sunk what little was left of his inheritance into supporting Dr. Griffiths's and his methods and, when that had run out, he'd applied to his brother...who had assumed he wanted funds for some unspecified debauchery. And thus, his litany of lies to source funds had been born.

"Or when you wished to oversee the shipping concern. Or when you studied botany. Or when you thought a life of academia would suit. You tried all these things, and none of them suited. There is nothing about this latest endeavour that makes me believe it will be any different. You have approached me with an idea, not a proposal. I have nothing against ideas, Stephen, but substance is required. Reports. Evidence. Christ, the reason you are even interested. You have offered none of these."

Staring to the side, Stephen tensed his jaw and recited in his head what he'd actually used the funds for. More funds for Dr. Griffiths. Assisting various parishes with purchasing school books and supplies. Establishment of a charity to provide clothing and essentials to unfortunates in London's slums. But Oliver had never seen any of those ventures and, clearly, had no desire to look. "Then, there is nothing more to say."

"There is more. Bring me the evidence. A plan. Show these funds will not be wasted. I do not wish to keep you from pursuing your interests, but there has to be some basis."

Stephen's lips twisted. "And there it is. You believe me frivolous." Funny, he would have thought that observation had long since lost the power to hurt.

Oliver cursed. "Stephen..."

There was no point steering the conversation to the charity today. Oliver clearly believed he would use the funds ill and would not bleed a single penny. "I shall bother you no longer. Good afternoon, Roxwaithe." Shooting to his feet, he stormed to the door.

"Brother, do not—" The words faded as Stephen wrenched the door shut behind him, stomping down the hall for good measure. Let Oliver stew on their argument. Let him feel guilt and castigate himself for his harshness. His brother deserved to feel all that and more. Then, in a few days or a week, Stephen would return the penitent and agree that yes, Oliver was correct, the spiritual study was a terrible idea. However, he did have this new desire to help with a charity for the education of young persons using the lure of football...

Heading back down the servant stairs, he made his way again to the kitchen. Mrs Parsons still worked with dough, her cheek decorated with a streak of flour. Her expression turned worried. "Oh, Lord, you and your brother have upset each other, haven't you?"

Abruptly, the tension he hadn't realised he'd been carrying crashed over him. Shoulders slumping, he ran a hand over his face. "When do we not?"

Mrs Parsons shook her head. "I don't understand. You were so close as boys. You and him and...Lord Maxim." At the mention of his younger brother, her voice broke.

He watched her sniff and wipe at her eyes. "We grew into men who dislike each other, I suppose." Although Maxim didn't have a chance to grow to manhood. His eyes burned, but ruthlessly he forced the emotion aside.

A breath shuddered through Mrs Parsons. "Well, be sure to inform that man at your rooms Simon will be by with another basket tomorrow."

Grateful for the change of subject, he smiled wanly. "You're too good to me, Mrs Parsons."

Her already pink cheeks darkened. "Cor, be away with you, boy. And mind your brother. You're as bad as each other."

Stephen saluted her as he walked out the servant's entrance. Perhaps they were as bad as each other, but it was obvious things were never going to change. Oliver would always think him unworthy. The amusing thing was, he was rather certain Oliver was right.

***

HEART RACING, STEPHEN WOKE with a start. Gulping air, he vaulted upright, running his hands over his chest, his hips, his legs. There were no splints, no bandages, and agony didn't scream through his body with every movement. He was in his own bed, not lying in a broken, upturned carriage somewhere in France. It was dark, as it had been that night, but there was no rain, no mud.

Leaning forward, he placed his head in his hands. Christ. He didn't have those nightmares often anymore, but when he did, they terrified him. And they weren't really nightmares, were they?

He felt again the weight of the broken seat pinning his leg and hips, the dull throb of pain that he'd later discovered had been a bad break in both legs and a fractured hip. Again, he saw Harbor opposite, half-obscured by the planks jutting from the broken carriage floor. He'd been covered in blood and still. So still. Hours they'd remained so, Stephen pinned while Harbor remained still, and he'd kept talking, kept repeating they were going to be found and they would laugh about it over a snifter of brandy even as he was horribly afraid he was talking to himself. That Harbor was gone.

Well, he was gone, wasn't he?

Swiping at the wetness on his cheeks, he hauled himself out of bed. He knew from experience he would not sleep again that night. Might as well get some work done.

Lighting the lamp at his bedside, he made his way to the desk piled high with plans and papers. Pushing all memory of the nightmare aside, he instead immersed himself in schematics and strategies and tried to forget again that awful night his best friend had died.

Chapter Five

Sinking another ball into the billiard table's pocket, Stephen straightened and reached for the cue chalk. He'd been at the 1810 Club for over an hour, sinking balls and perfecting his technique. Outside the door, he'd heard it slowly become rowdier, the club becoming busier as the night grew later and gentlemen arrived in pursuit of pleasure after familial obligations had been met.

Moving around the table, he lined up his next shot. The cue was unbalanced in his hand, the shaft too short and the weight slightly off. He could have brought his own cue, tailored to his height and weighted to his grip while sporting the very finest leather tip, but he preferred to employ this inferior cue on occasion if only to force him to employ greater skill to compensate.

Just as he was about the execute the shot, the door banged open. His shot went wide, bouncing off the cushion and careening wildly across the baize.

"Told you he was hiding here," the Honourable Charles Montford announced.

"Yes, yes, you're very clever." Viscount Pinet pushed his way into the room. The viscount wore one of the most absurd waistcoats Stephen had ever seen and that, as Pinet regularly garbed himself in truly horrendous waistcoats, was saying something. "Were you hiding yourself, Farlisle?"

Leaning on his cue, he scowled. "If I were, I did a piss-poor job of it."

Pinet sniffed as he flopped into the room's sole armchair.

"Please, do make yourself at home," Stephen said.

Hooking his leg over the arm, Pinet flicked at an invisible piece of lint on his lapel. "Thank you, I shall."

Montford, meanwhile, was chalking his own cue. "Are we playing for anything?"

"*I* was playing to enhance my skill. Alone," he said pointedly.

"How fortunate for you, then, that I should arrive to assist you," Montford said, blithely unconcerned by Stephen's ire.

"I wished an evening to myself, Montford."

"All your evenings are to yourself. If you truly wished that, you would have stayed home."

"You would think the fact I didn't seek any of you out would have been a hint that perhaps I wanted to be alone."

Montford smiled blandly. "You would think that."

Stephen looked between them. A sinking feeling began in his stomach. "So if you're here, does that mean—"

The door swung open. Mr Connor Fairfax entered, quickly followed by the Earl of Ashburton and—bloody hell, that was half his luck. Bringing up the rear was the bloody Duke of Sutton. "Excellent. You're all here," Stephen said sourly.

"Kind of you to reserve a room for us, old man," Fairfax said, clapping him on his bad shoulder.

Stephen winced. "As I was saying, I aimed for solitude—"

"Lucky you have us, then, to break it for you." Ash scowled at Fairfax. "Don't clip him on that wing, Fairfax. That's the one that's broke."

"Brok-*en*." Sutton shook his head. "Bloody hell, Ashburton, anyone would think you were raised in the gutter with the way you speak."

"I beg your pardon, Your Grace. Not all of us can be as perfect as yourself."

Sutton, prig that he was, declined to answer.

Stephen looked among them. Somehow, these five disparate men had become his closest friends, all because of Harbor and his Will. Well, all were his friends bar Sutton. He doubted anyone would call Sutton their friend.

The six of them had not really known each other prior to Harbor bequeathing them the 1810 Club. They attended Rugby together, and then Cambridge, but Stephen would have only ever accounted them as acquaintances. Harbor was the one who had been friendly with them, and his Will had bestowed joint ownership upon them all, stipulating they must meet at least monthly to discuss the stewardship of the club. At first, they had met for those monthly meetings only, but slowly they had met outside the meetings, and then they had met for amusement. Now, it seemed they were determined to plague him with alarming regularity, ruining his tendency to solitary pursuits.

"Tell Montford he's bloody terrible at billiards and should hang up his cue." Pinet said, examining his nails.

"I'm not terrible," Montford protested mildly. "I'm merely discerning."

"You're terrible," Fairfax said flatly. A big man with craggy features, his huge hands dwarfed the billiard balls he racked.

"Et tu, Fairfax?"

Fairfax grunted and continued to set the table.

Stephen leaned on his cue as Montford and Fairfax argued over the scoring system. Well, Montford argued while Fairfax stared at him mutely. Pinet continued to groom himself while Sutton arranged himself against the wall, observing all of them with that superior look on his face.

"We haven't really disturbed you, have we?" Ash said, coming to stand beside him.

"Would you all leave if I said yes?"

Ash grinned. "No."

"Then what does it matter?" Stephen asked ruefully.

Ash's grin faded into a comfortable smile. Montford and Fairfax had finally commenced their game, and Stephen and Ash watched as they ratcheted up the competitiveness.

"When next do you have a football game?" Ash asked.

Gaze on the play before them, Stephen said distractedly, "Saturday." Then, realising what Ash had asked, he looked at his friend sharply. "I do *not* require a cheer squad."

"But you have a ready-made one," Ash wheedled.

He exhaled. "Leave it be, Ash."

"I don't know why you insist on this solitary life, Farlisle. You know none of us will allow it."

He grunted.

Shaking his head, Ash continued, "In any event, I'll be at your game on Saturday, though it *is* rather lowering to attend such a common pastime."

"Then don't."

"Ah, Farlisle. The more you say such things, the greater

my desire to attend." Ash grinned.

"You're a prat."

"Yes. Yes, I am."

"Saw Seraphina Waller-Mitchell sniffing around you at the Pruitt ball."

Both Stephen and Ash whirled their gazes around. Sutton had not moved from the wall, his gaze levelled upon them.

Frowning, Stephen said, "What?"

Sutton took a sip from the glass in his hand. "Lady Seraphina. Took quite the interest in you."

He exchanged a look with Ash. The earl shrugged. "So?" Stephen asked.

Sutton swirled his glass. "Surely you've heard."

"Heard what?" he said impatiently. While he might tease Ash about being a prat, Sutton actually was one.

"I, too, am intrigued by this pronouncement." Ash said.

"Every year, Seraphina Waller-Mitchell selects a gentlemen to pursue her."

"So?"

"So, it seems this year, she's selected you. She's taken her time this year." He raked his gaze over Stephen. "Perhaps she finds something of interest in you."

Studying Sutton, Ash finally said, "Last year, didn't she choose you?"

Anger flared in Sutton's eyes before he quashed it. "We chose each other. She was amusing for a time." Sutton levelled his gaze on Stephen. "She will have you wrapped around her finger before a fortnight has passed."

Christ, what did he care? They had spoken for less than ten minutes, and it had been clear she'd had a game in mind. While he'd been tempted for a moment, he had left such things behind years ago. Let her choose him. It didn't mean he had to play his part.

Sutton pointed at him. "A hundred pounds she has you panting after her by mid-September."

Seriously? He wished a wager? "You do realise this is juvenile?"

"The betting books are filled with pettier wagers. Do you agree?"

"For a hundred pounds where I can completely control the outcome? Certainly." If Sutton wanted to throw his money away, he wasn't going to stop him. A hundred pounds would pay a half-dozen foundation administrators' wages for a year.

"Can't just avoid her, though. In fact, let's make this interesting. You have to court her."

"Fine."

"And, if you can get her to show a marked preference for you, I'll even throw in an extra hundred."

Stephen stared at him. "You would have me toy with her emotions."

Sutton smiled thinly. "Two hundred pounds, Farlisle."

In the background, Fairfax and Montford argued over who'd scored the most points while Pinet still lounged in the armchair. Two hundred pounds. He could do a lot with two hundred pounds, but the thought of manipulating the emotions of the intriguing woman with the cat's eyes and magnificent bosom left him with an astringent taste. But, two hundred pounds... "I agree, Sutton."

"By the end of the season, you'll be completely enthralled by her, devastated and weeping, and I'll collect my hundred pounds. Or, you'll have *her* devastated and weeping, and you'll be two hundred pounds richer."

"If you say so."

Sutton nodded. "I shall enter it in the betting book. If you will excuse me." Executing a sharp bow, he strode through the door.

Ash caught Stephen's arm. "This is a bad idea. When has a wager of this nature ever turned out well? You're involving someone else, without her consent or consideration of how she will feel. Are you sure you are willing to bear the consequences?"

He shrugged.

Disappointment shaped Ash's features. "Can't say I didn't warn you."

"No. You can't." And then, because he did like Ash, he gave a half-smile. "Trust me, Ash."

"You have a plan?"

"Half of one. The rest will come to me." He lifted his cue. "Now, shall we trounce Montford and Fairfax at billiards?"

Chapter Six

ARMS CROSSED OVER HIS chest, Stephen trained his gaze on the ballroom's entrance. He'd arrived over an hour ago, situating himself at his current vantage and setting to wait for Lady Seraphina's arrival. Though she had yet to make her entrance, he counted his time well spent, if only for the observations he'd made thus far.

A contessa—he could not recall the name to go with the title and would no doubt mangle it in any event as his Italian was shocking—had stood impatiently for the majordomo to announce her and shot him a haughty look once he did so. A group of young men had loitered near the entrance, elbowing and jostling each other as each young debutante entered the ballroom to join her friends in giggling and casting surreptitious glances their way. Finally, one youth, spurred on by his friends, separated from the pack and approach one of the young ladies. Puffing up his chest, he'd bowed low over her hand and asked something, most likely to dance. The girl had dissolved into giggles, as did her friends, but she'd blushingly accepted and, with a triumphant smile at his peers, the young man led her to the dance floor.

A faint smile curved his lips. A dozen years ago, that could have been him and Harb—

Cutting off the thought before it could form, he swallowed past the lump in his throat.

Deliberately, he turned his focus to the ballroom entrance. There was no clock in view, but it had to be approaching eleven o'clock, and he hadn't eschewed society long enough not to know arriving fashionably late was raison d'être to some. Lady Seraphina Waller-Mitchell, it seemed, was included in that number.

"The Earl of Ashburton."

Gaze avid, Ash almost skipped down the stairs. Ash loved a ball and didn't care who knew it. If Stephen looked for him in an hour, Ash would be escorting yet another lady to a dance, his love of it well known.

Subtly, Stephen crouched behind a well-placed potted plant, obscuring himself from Ash. He didn't need questions or condemnations or the faint hint of disapproval this evening: He had a plan, and he had a mind to execute it.

"Stephen."

Bloody hell, he had sought to avoid the disapproval of one man and instead fell prey to another. Grimacing and not bothering to disguise it, he turned. "Oliver," he greeted his brother.

Arms crossed over his broad chest, Oliver frowned. "I did not expect to see you here."

"Nor did I expect to see you." He smiled thinly. "It seems we surprise each other."

His brother exhaled. "Can you not be civil for a half a second, Stephen?"

"I don't know. Can you?"

Shaking his head, Oliver said, "Like that, is it?"

Clenching his jaw, he averted his gaze and undertook his level best to ignore his brother. Why was he even here? Oliver barely attended society events, preferring instead to shut himself away in his study and play about with paper and numbers until it was time to slumber, only to rise the next day and perform the same tedious tasks again.

"How goes your studies?"

Stephen jerked his head around. "What?"

Oliver's lips thinned. "Your studies into the spiritual, the curriculum you were so passionate about not three days past."

"Oh, that." He waved a hand. "A mere fancy."

"A fancy," Oliver repeated. His eyes narrowed. "How much debt do you carry?"

Stephen's hackles rose. "What?"

"How much, Stephen? How many creditors should I expect to darken the doors of Roxegate with requests to settle your accounts?"

"I am the son of an earl. I do not need to pay for things." Bedamned if he told Oliver he held not one debt. He may have been a spendthrift and reckless in his youth, but he'd learned his goddamned lesson, and he'd learned it hard. Oliver, though, never saw him as anything but a profligate and wastrel, and Stephen couldn't be bothered to correct him.

Oliver sighed. "Do you require your debts settled?" he asked reluctantly.

"If I should ever accrue debts that require settling, you may be assured you will be the first person I contact." And then, just to agitate his brother, he said, "What do you know of Egypt?"

Alarm lit Oliver's eyes. "Egypt? Why?"

"No reason." Idly, he surveyed the crowd. Let his brother stew on that one and imagine the worst. Stephen had no intention of anything with Egypt, but the opportunity to fluster his pompous, controlling brother was irresistible.

"The Marchioness of Demartine, Lady Alexandra Torrence, and Lady Lydia Torrence," the majordomo announced.

Beside him, Oliver tensed.

Stephen's lips twisted. Ah, the reason for his brother's attendance was finally clear.

It was a poorly kept secret that Lydia loved Oliver and he her, and when Stephen was younger, he'd placed numerous bets with Lydia's brothers over when they would actually declare themselves and wed. The only thing standing in their way— which was utter nonsense—was Oliver's insistence he was too old. Fourteen years separated them, but men older than Oliver married women younger than Lydia all the bloody time. His brother was being stubborn and stupid, but then Oliver was often stubborn and stupid.

Now that Lydia had arrived, he would wager a hefty sum his brother would not hear a word he now said. "I have heard there are many wonders to behold in Egypt," he commented, if only to prove his theory correct.

"Hmm." His brother's gaze did not leave Lydia.

No outrage. No disappointed glance. "Hieroglyphics and the like. Pharaohs and such. Perhaps a visit is in order," Stephen said, enjoying himself immensely.

"Perhaps," Oliver said distractedly "Excuse me, brother." And with that, Oliver strode after Lydia.

Smirking, he watched his brother trail after the girl he claimed he had not more than avuncular feeling for.

"Lady Seraphina Waller-Mitchell."

Glove skimming the balustrade, Seraphina Waller-Mitchell descended the stairs. In her other hand she held her fan, positioned just beneath the décolletage of her deep blue gown. The colour offset the creaminess of her skin, the graceful sweep of her neck, and highlighted her impressive cleavage. Her dark hair was twisted in complicated knots and curls, shining in the candlelight as did the diamonds dripping from her ears.

Conversation ceased as she continued her descent, her appearance commanding every eye. Gaze downcast, a demure smile played about her rose-pink lips, as if she were embarrassed by the attention.

It was quite a performance, though he did concede she *was* stunning.

As she reached the gathered throng, a lord stepped forward and offered his arm. From his vantage, Stephen couldn't see who it was, but Seraphina accepted him and allowed him to escort her in the direction of the ballroom.

Pushing off the wall, he made his way to her. "Lady Seraphina," he said, bowing before her.

Her dazzling smile did not dim, but the skin around her eyes tightened. "Lord Stephen, what a delight to see you this evening. This is Lord Stephen Farlisle who interrupts us, Lord Bancroft. He is brother to the Earl of Roxwaithe. We met at the Pruitt ball where he saved me from that most direst of fates: a torn hem. Lord Stephen, do you know Lord Bancroft?"

His jaw tensed. Something about how she said his name set his teeth on edge. "I do not." Shifting his gaze to the man at her side, he nodded. "Bancroft."

"Lord Stephen. A pleasure, I am sure."

Stephen smiled without mirth. A more enthused utterance of those words he could not imagine. "Lady Seraphina, I would speak with you if you would grant me the honour."

Sliding her gaze over him, she fluttered her fan. "I will speak with you if you ask me to dance," she said archly.

Annoyance tensed his muscles, but he did as she bid. "Lady Seraphina, may I have this dance?"

"I must check if I am free." She made a show of consulting her dance card. Moments passed, one sliding into the next as he resisted the urge to shift his weight impatiently while

Lord Bancroft glared at him from her side.

Finally, his impatience got the better of him. "Lady Seraphina."

Eyes on her dance card, she said, "Yes, Lord Stephen?"

It took all he had not to grit his teeth. "May I have this dance?"

Dropping her card, she smiled prettily as she held out her gloved hand. "You may." She flicked her gaze to Lord Bancroft. "I shall be back shortly."

The man spluttered impotently as Stephen led her to the dance floor. As they lined up with the other dancers, the orchestra began the first strains of a quadrille.

Holding up a hand to execute the first move, he asked without preamble, "What do you want?"

She missed a step, offering an apologetic smile to the dancer she stumbled into. "I beg your pardon?" she asked from the corner of her mouth.

"From me," he clarified. "What do you want from me?"

Her demure smile didn't falter. "I'm sure I don't know to what you refer."

"You know very well to what I refer."

Still smiling, he watched as she very deliberately stepped on her gown, causing her to again stumble. "Oh dear," she cried.

"What is it?"

"I've turned my ankle. Will you escort me to the retiring room?"

His lips twitched. How very convenient. "Of course, Lady Seraphina."

She limped rather convincingly as he helped her leave the ballroom in favour of the room set aside for ladies to gather themselves. Glancing about them and finding them quite alone, she tugged him into another room, this one dark and unoccupied.

He glanced about the room with interest. "I had no idea this room was here."

Turning, she scowled. "What do you think you're about?"

Ah, there was the woman he remembered from the Pruitt's ball. "You seem to desire my attention."

"You think highly of yourself."

He shrugged.

"Why would I want your attention, when you've so clearly demonstrated you don't wish to give it?"

"I don't know. That's why I asked you."

She crossed her arms, drawing his gaze to her impressive breasts. They pushed against her bodice, full and round and soft. They looked more than a handful, and his palm itched to cover them, to discover if they were more than *his* handful.

He jerked his gaze up.

She smirked at him, as if she knew every single one of his licentious thoughts. "And why do you want to know?"

Clearing his throat, he said, "Because I've made a wager."

She blinked. "A wager."

"I require your cooperation to win it."

Arms still crossed, she studied him. "Perhaps you'd better tell me of this wager," she finally said.

"That I won't fall to your charms."

Her jaw dropped. "I beg your pardon?"

"The Duke of Sutton has wagered one hundred pounds I will succumb. I have wagered I won't. It is not a matter of simply avoiding you; I must be seen to engage with you."

Expression unchanged, she stared at him. He had no idea what she made of this. "I mean to win this wager, Lady Seraphina. He then wagered a further one hundred pounds if I can instead gain your devotion. That two hundred pounds will do more good in my hands than in Sutton's."

She gave a sharp laugh. "You are to entrap *me*?"

"As I said. I did not much like the thought of deceiving you, and thus our conversation."

Tilting her head, he could see her considering his words. "The Duke of Sutton made this wager, you say?"

"He did."

"How very spiteful of him." She exhaled. "I do not know what to think."

"I have no wish to trick you, or to lie to you. I prefer your cooperation."

"Yes, I can see that for myself. Let me think."

He remained silent as she paced, her fingers to her temple.

"What do I have to gain from this?"

"The knowledge you are doing good?"

"How am I doing good?"

After concealing the truth of his philanthropy for so long, he found himself now without words to explain. He stared at her mutely.

She waved a hand. "No matter. I shall do this, if only so I can frustrate Sutton's plans. He will rue the day he chose to toy with me by the time I am through with him." At his surprise, she smiled maliciously. "I never claimed *I* wasn't spiteful."

A venomous glint still lit her eyes, her full pink lips twisted still in the malevolent grin. Unease slid down his spine, but he ignored any misgivings. "Do we have a deal?"

Focus turning to him, the vindictiveness in her expression disappeared. "Yes, Lord Stephen. We do."

"Excellent. We should formulate a plan—"

"*I* shall formulate a plan. I shall inform you of it once it is complete. It shouldn't take more than…three days."

He cared not who produced the plan, only that one was. Holding out his hand, he said, "It is settled."

She stared at his offered appendage. Finally, with a sigh, she took it.

Gloves, both hers and his, prevented them from sealing this deal skin to skin. The fingers that slid into his hand were slender, and he wished he could feel her flesh, the caress of her palm against his, the warmth of her skin. Grey eyes locked with his, framed by dark lashes. His breath locked in his chest, the room about them fading as he fell into her gaze.

He didn't know how long they stood there.

Abruptly, the strains of a waltz swirled through the room. Clearing her throat, she pulled her hand from his, her tongue darting to wet her lips. "We should return to the dancing."

Her mouth was luscious, her lips deep pink and full. He wondered if they tasted sweet, if they were as soft and plump as they looked.

He shook himself. "Yes," he said, his voice cracking.

She took his arm and they slipped back into the hall. No one had noted their absence, the dance floor still crowded, those not dancing chattering, gossiping and laughing. They took a turn around the room, Lady Seraphina's fingers digging into his forearm to direct him in one direction or another. He didn't care much one way or another where they went, so he allowed her imperiousness.

"Tell me true, do I have something on my face?"

At the arbitrary question, his brows rose. Glancing at her, he said, "No. Why?"

"That girl stares at me."

Following her direction, his gaze lit on a dark-haired girl

with rich brown skin. Her face lit with a smile when she saw their attention. "Who is she?"

Brows knitted, Lady Seraphina dug her fingers again into his arm. Following her prompt, he turned them to the right. "A Miss Edirisinghe from Ceylon. Several times I have caught her gaze."

"Perhaps you should talk to her. Ask her what it is that draws her attention."

Shocked eyes swung to him. "Why on earth should I do that?" she said, her tone aghast.

"So you may discover what she wants." It seemed obvious to him.

"Oh. Oh my." She cocked her head. "You are a bit simple, aren't you?"

Perhaps he was, but asking the girl was the most direct method to discover what fascinated her so. "Ask her, or don't. It is your choice."

Stopping stock still, she stared at him. He had no notion why. Finally, a smile played about her lips. "You surprise me, Lord Stephen. I am surprised."

"By what?"

"Most men would insist they know best and direct me to follow their demand."

Not knowing how to reply, he shrugged.

"As I said, I am surprised." Lifting her hand from his arm, she said "In three days, then?"

As what he wanted to discuss with her was over, he had no concern her words were a dismissal. Taking her hand and bowing low, he murmured. "In three days." He allowed his lips to brush ever-so-slightly over her gloved knuckles.

The slightest intake of breath. Reclaiming her hand, she curtsied and then swept into the crowd. Staring after her, he allowed a smile. It seemed he could also affect her.

Three days. Was it strange he was looking forward to it?

Chapter Seven

Leaving behind her coachman and barouche, Sera trudged across the heath. This was beyond the pale. Her half-boots were becoming water-logged, and Delphine grumbled as she followed behind her, curses in her native French that Sera shouldn't understand. She agreed with her maid's sentiments precisely. This was not what she expected when she set out this morning.

Ahead, men raced around the heath chasing after a ball. One man kicked it through white posts, causing raucous cheer from those on the field and the smattering of spectators surrounding the play.

She could not, however, see Lord Stephen.

His valet had informed her Lord Stephen took exercise on the heath at this time on Tuesday afternoons, but all she could see were men and boys running around after a ball. She knew not how old the boys were, but they were all arms and legs, as if their bodies had gained height but their limbs had not quite worked out the knack of it. There were no gentlemanly pursuits, such as boxing or fencing or, at a stretch, shooting. Where on earth was Lord Stephen?

The players on the heath did something with the ball to rouse another cheer from the spectators. She studied them. She had no idea what was going on. They were…passing the ball to each other by kicking it. Why did not one of them pick up the ball and run with it?

Across the field, a player charged at the one moving the ball along the ground at high speed. Using his shoulder and hip, he bumped the player on his side, causing the other player to stumble but he did not relinquish the ball. The one who had charged bumped him again, and then again, and this time when the other player stumbled, he stole possession of the ball. With a sharp, straight kick, he passed it to another player, and then every man and boy switched direction, running towards the white poles on the opposite side of the field. Not more than thirty feet from the goal, the player with possession of the ball struck it with a sharp strike. The ball sailed past the player who desperately defended the space, barely clearing the left post. The players went wild, celebrating. Perhaps that was a score?

His back to her, the player who had stolen the ball had slowed to a steady jog. Others in his team gathered him in their exuberance, jumping in an embrace of four or more. Ruefully shaking his head, the player extracted himself and turned, his face split by a wide grin.

She blinked. Good heavens. It was Lord Stephen. Never had she seen him express such joy. She'd seen a half-smile, a smirk, the faint curving of his lips, but never so broad a smile.

Her gaze travelled over him. He wore no waistcoat or coat, his necktie had long been abandoned, and his shirt was open at his throat, displaying a strong column of smooth, golden flesh. Though tall and broad shouldered, in the ballroom he appeared angular and gangly, the garb of a gentleman disguising the lean muscle of his chest and arms. His thighs were strong and powerful, thick muscle flexing as he turned on the field, racing at speed to pursue the player with the ball. His shirt outlined the long muscles in his back, and his behind was round, hard with muscle and—

She cleared her throat. Why on *earth* was she staring at Lord Stephen's behind?

A whistle sounded, and the players came to a standstill, some clapping each other on the back, some jostling and ribbing each other. Lord Stephen did not engage in the celebrations. One man motioned for him to do so, but Lord Stephen only smiled and did not join the group, instead making his way toward the sidelines. As he approached, his gaze lit upon her. Raising a hand in greeting, the corner of his mouth lifted and he picked up his pace, jogging to her. Sweat darkened his hair at the temples, the strands standing every which way.

He executed a sharp bow. "Lady Seraphina."

Dipping a curtsey, she greeted him in kind. "Lord Stephen."

"I am surprised to see you. It is not often a lady wanders

on to the heath."

She lifted her chin. "You did not attend me."

Surprise lit his face briefly. "When did I not attend you?"

"I sent a note yesterday morning outlining our next meet and asking for an immediate response. You did not respond."

He ran his hand through his damp hair, the muscles in his forearm flexing. Her mouth went dry. "I did not receive it. My apologies."

Wetting her lips, she admonished herself for such an appalling reaction. He was ungarbed, dishevelled, and less like a gentleman she could not imagine. She should be disgusted. "What do you do here?"

Deadpan, he said, "Play football."

"Yes, I can see you play that...game. But why are *you* here?"

He crossed his arms over his chest. "Because I enjoy it."

A dark-haired lad ran up, all arms and legs and gangly besides. "Lord Stephen, we are setting up another match. You will play, yes?" A faint accent coloured his words, the cadence slightly off.

Lord Stephen grunted, tipping his chin up in affirmation. "Tell the other lads I'll be there shortly."

The boy beamed. "Yes, sir," he said, and then ran back to the field. As he did so, he passed another player who was making his way toward them. The man said something to the boy to make him grin and then continued toward them.

Sera glanced at Lord Stephen as the man approached. The slightest of frowns touched his brow, but he said nothing as the man joined them. He was handsome, with a lean, rangy build, and sweat had made damp curls of his dark hair, wrecked by his fingers into sticking and standing from his skull in turn. His skin was tanned golden by the sun, and his features boasted a strong, aquiline nose while an easy grin pulled at his full lips.

"Greetings, my lady. It is a delight to have you at our training." His words were coloured with the same accent as the boy. "It would be a delight also to have your acquaintance, if this surly chap will introduce us."

Sera hid a smile as the man grinned at Lord Stephen.

"Franco, this is Lady Seraphina Waller-Mitchell. Lady Seraphina, Senor Christopher Franco," Lord Stephen said flatly.

"Mr Franco, if you please. We are in England."

Lord Stephen glanced at Mr Franco. "Since when do you

refer to yourself as such?"

"My father and mother may claim Italy and Campania as their birthplace, but I was born here, Farlisle." Mr Franco turned his dazzling smile on Sera. "My lady, are you here to donate?"

Lord Stephen's frown turned ferocious. "Franco, that is not why—"

"We can show you more of our programme, if you give me a moment to make myself presentable." Grinning, he gestured at Lord Stephen. "His lordship here, too."

Glancing between them, she returned Mr Franco's smile even as her thoughts raced. "Your programme?"

"Our charity receives patronage from some of the most prestigious people in the Ton, as I'm sure Lord Stephen has already informed you. I am certain, however, a lady such as yourself does not require my opinion when it is clear you are more than capable of forming your own."

Mr Franco was very charming, flattering in the right places, deferential in others. No doubt he won many a patron to his side with his charisma, and his roguish grin would have the ladies flocking to bask in his glow and, she was certain, to his bed. "Mr Franco, do you find such an approach often works? I imagine you apply such flattery frequently."

For a moment, he stared at her, then he burst out in laughter. "I do, Lady Seraphina," he said. "Has it worked with you?"

"Perhaps. I will discuss it with my man of business, in any event. Being charitable is our duty and our privilege, do you not think?"

"I do." He turned an amused glance on Lord Stephen. "You didn't bring her here for the charity, did you?"

"I didn't bring her here at all," Lord Stephen said sourly.

"*Va bene.*" He looked at Lord Stephen. "*Mi dispiace*, my friend."

Lord Stephen shrugged.

"I shall leave you now. As I said, a delight to meet you, Lady Seraphina."

"And you, Mr Franco." She gave him her prettiest smile.

Amusement lit his features. He glanced at Lord Stephen. "Good luck."

Lord Stephen grunted.

With another dazzling smile, Mr Franco bowed and departed.

As Mr Franco rejoined those on the field, Sera turned to Lord Stephen. "A charity?"

His hands tightened on his biceps. "As Franco said."

She digested this. She had heard nothing of Lord Stephen's involvement with a charity and, if Maria and Elizabeth could not discover it, it meant he kept it very quiet indeed. "And what is this charity?"

He exhaled. "None of your concern."

"It is my concern, if I am to contribute to it."

He shot her a dark look. "You do not have to prevaricate for my benefit. Clearly, Franco could think of no other reason you would be here."

"Your conquests do not often come to quiver and sigh over your physical prowess?"

His gaze sharpened. "Is that what you were doing? Quivering and sighing?"

Abruptly, she realised she had lost control of this conversation. "You run a charity?" she said instead.

He stared at her a moment, clearly torn. "I do," he finally said.

"What is it?"

The tension drained from his body. "This one is to increase literacy and school attendance in factory children."

She blinked. This one? "How?"

"We run a football league where participation is contingent on attending a certain number of hours of schooling. We also realise if children attend school, they are not earning wages for their family, so we pay them what they would have earned if they were working."

Astonishment locked her jaw. He was— That— "This is what you want Sutton's money for?"

He nodded sharply.

"Why did I know none of this?" she asked, almost to herself.

"The Ton is interested in pleasure, not toil."

Hackles rising, she whipped her gaze to his.

Before she opened her mouth to defend herself, he said, "I mean no offence. We are raised to care of little but our own pleasure, especially if we are not a first-born son." His lips twisted. "I know my father did not care to impress upon me the importance of duty to one's fellow man."

Studying him, she said slowly, "And you have found this

approach successful?"

He nodded once. "We've had a significant increase in school attendance, but we always require funds, hence my attendance at balls and gatherings. We must go where the money is." He grimaced. "That reminds me."

"Reminds you of what?"

"I must see my brother." He straightened. "So, you wished to see me?

Belatedly, she recalled the reason she had trudged out on this heath. The reason he had *forced* her to trudge out on the heath. Hiding her scowl, she opened her reticule and withdrew a folded sheaf of paper. "I have determined a plan for our courtship. As you can see, I have drawn up a schedule."

Taking the sheaf, he leafed through it. "This is…comprehensive."

She lifted her chin. "Of course. I am nothing if not thorough."

"Thursday, three o'clock in the afternoon. Escort Lady Seraphina to Liddle's Tea Shop," he read. "Thursday, half three in the afternoon. Escort to Merriweather's Book Emporium." He raised his gaze to hers. "Only half an hour for an ice?"

"You will find all items allotted in thirty-minute increments."

The corner of his mouth lifted. "Will I?"

"I find determining a unit of measurement helpful when planning. Thirty minutes seemed most effective—enough time to be noticed, not too much to be the subject of speculation."

Almost smiling, he shook his head. "I cannot argue with that."

"Look over my schedule. If you have any conflicts, mark them and return to me."

He glanced at the paper. "Tonight I shall see you at the Canton-Smythe musicale?"

"You shall."

"Excellent." He smiled, widely and with genuine amusement. As he did on the field.

Her breath strangled in her chest. When he smiled, he was…dazzling. Overwhelmed, she fought to conceal her reaction, to maintain the fiction she was unaffected. But she was affected. Horribly.

"I will see you again this evening, Lady Seraphina," he said, his smile fading to a warm glow. He gave no indication he had noticed her distraction. Thank goodness.

"If we are to pretend courtship, you must call me Seraphina," she said, pretending now herself composed.

"Seraphina." His rough voice caressed her name.

A shiver ran through her. What on earth was wrong with her? This could not be tolerated. "And I may call you Stephen?"

The corner of his mouth kicked up again. "You may." Someone called his name from the field. "I must go," he said.

"Of course."

"Until this evening, Seraphina." Again he caressed her name.

Unable to speak, she nodded.

With another enigmatic smile, he turned and rejoined the field.

She watched him go, her heart racing. His shirt still highlighted the lines of his back, and her mouth dried as he performed a stretch that pushed the long muscles against the cloth—

Hastily, she turned and made her way back to her carriage. The less she thought on a rumpled and dishevelled Lord Stephen, the better.

Chapter Eight

Sera resisted the urge to take her watch from her pocket and check it again. It was only two after the hour. Lord Stephen was not late enough as yet to warrant annoyance. At least, that was what she told herself. She was, in fact, annoyed. Vastly.

The street was bustling with afternoon traffic, and the tea shop was quickly filling up. She'd had Delphine reserve a table, and even now her maid sat at that table to ensure none would presume to think it available, a scowl and a torrent of angry French scaring away those who dared approach.

Her watch burned a hole in her pocket. They had attended the Canton-Smythe musicale two evenings previous, as per her plan. He'd been amiable and attentive, and any who observed would be hard pressed to assume anything other than the beginnings of a courtship between them. She'd even spied the Duke of Sutton spying on *them*, his mouth tight with annoyance. Pleased, she'd turned her cheek and pretended not to notice his ire, laughing and touching Lord Stephen's arm to dig salt into the duke's wounds.

Stephen now finally strode toward her, and she cast a critical eye. His clothing was better fitting and more fashionable than the garb he wore to the ball and the musicale, as if the more formal attire was less often employed and thus not as often replaced. Buckskin breeches outlined his powerful thighs more ably than those he'd worn to the ball, the material clinging lovingly to every muscle. A sable-brown coat stretched over his broad shoulders, and now she knew the shape of the arms beneath, it seemed obvious to her the strength in his lean frame. The tall hat concealed most of his blond hair, though pomade slicked the strands curled around his ears. He moved with confidence, light on his feet, and she could see the influence of the hours he spent on a football field in his every step.

"Lady Seraphina." He halted before her, bowing sharply.

She was going to respond in kind but instead what came out was, "You're late."

The corner of his mouth tipped up. "My apologies, I know that disturbs your schedule. We won't have the full half-hour for ices."

"No, we won't." She arched her brow. "See that it doesn't happen again."

Still wearing that slight smile, he nodded solemnly as he held out his arm. "Shall we?"

Wrapping her fingers around his forearm, she allowed him to escort her into Liddle's Tea Shop.

Delphine did indeed sit at the table, baring her teeth at a gentleman who attempted to take the table. "Thank you, Delphine," Sera said. Turning an acid smile on the gentleman, she asked, "Did you wish something, sir?"

He balked. "No. I am sorry. I—" Hastily, he removed himself.

Stephen watched him leave. "Impressive," he said softly.

She ignored the thrill his approval gave her. "Delphine," she said to her maid. "You may order yourself an ice."

"*Merci*, my lady. I have long desired the tangerine."

Sera kept her expression mildly pleased. Tangerine. Ugh. "You may go, Delphine."

Shooting a fierce glare at Stephen, she made her way to the counter.

"Why did she glare at me?" he asked.

Taking her seat, Sera replied, "She is protective."

Amusement twisted his lips. "From what I've seen, you need little protection," he said as he also took his seat. After summoning a waiter and placing their order, he said, "What shall we talk about?"

She blinked. "I beg your pardon?"

"We are to sit here for the next—" He consulted his pocket watch. "Eighteen minutes. What shall we discuss?"

Mind blank, she stared at him. She had not thought that far. How could she not think that far? "It's lovely weather we're having," she said, and dared him to comment on such an inane attempt.

"Yes, lovely weather." Barking a laugh, the corner of his mouth kicked up further. "Surely we can do better than the weather?"

"Very well." While she was still marvelling she'd somehow wrangled a laugh out of him, she cast about for something to say. "Why did you choose the flavour you did?"

"Because I like it."

She frowned. "That is not very descriptive."

"No," he said, and did not continue.

Breath exploding in a huff, she said crossly, "You are very vexing."

Again, that slight smile. "I know."

The sight of that oh-so-slight smile did not cause her heart to race. It *didn't*. "Let us try this again. What flavour did you choose? Why do you like it? If you couldn't choose that one, what would be your second choice?"

"Lemon basil. Because it tastes tart and fresh. Most likely pistachio."

"I chose strawberry and rhubarb."

Staring at her, he rubbed his finger over his bottom lip. "And why did you choose strawberry and rhubarb?"

She smiled sweetly. "Because I like it."

He laughed.

She sat back, absurdly pleased she'd made him laugh. Twice.

In a bustle of activity, their ices were placed before them. The sweet aroma of strawberries teasing her nose, and her mouth watered in anticipation.

Opposite her, Stephen lifted a spoon laden with ice, opening his mouth just enough to allow it to enter. Full lips closed delicately around the metal, his eyes fluttering as he absorbed the taste. The fabric of his gloves stretched his knuckles, long fingers cradling the delicate spoon in his large hand. His throat moved as he swallowed, his tongue darting out to caress the last of the ice from the spoon.

She made a sound.

He paused mid-lick. "I beg your pardon?"

Her head felt thick, and a fierce pulse pounded deep within her. "What?"

"You made a noise."

"I— Nothing." Hastily, she lowered her gaze to her own ice, her heart racing. Good God. How could he make the eating of an ice so…so sensual?

"Are you not enjoying your ice?" He frowned. "You haven't touched it."

"How goes your charity?" she asked, mostly to distract him.

"Good." Still he frowned. "Thank you for your donation," he added belatedly.

Regally, she inclined her head. "You are very welcome."

"How did you organise funds so quickly?" He lifted his spoon again to his mouth.

Unwilling to be so affected again, she averted her gaze. "I have full control of the inheritance my mother left me. Apparently, she believed a woman should have wealth independent of any man in her life."

"Ah." He licked his spoon and she tried, very hard, not to notice every movement of his tongue. "It must be nice, to have such easy access to wealth."

"Did you not have an inheritance of your own?"

He nodded, acknowledging the truth she spoke. "I did. And, if you ask those who know, I squandered it."

The sheer bitterness of his words stopped her harsh rejoinder. "And if I asked you?" she finally said.

For a long moment, he stared at her. Then, he said, "Did you know I was in an accident?"

She could think of no reason to prevaricate. Slowly, she nodded.

He nodded also. "I was bedridden for two years. The only reason I now walk is blind luck: the physician who happened upon me had some radical notions and I was in no position to refuse his care. My prognosis was…not good. It was either submit to his wild theories or—" He swallowed. "They were going to amputate," he finished softly.

She could not tear her gaze from him. He—he had gone through that?

"After my flesh knitted, I could not move—not well, not as I did before. Dr. Griffiths had me exercise, he and his assistant manipulated my muscles, and in time and with a huge amount of work, I was able to walk. Now, if I don't exercise regularly, my muscles seize, the pain becomes worse, and I cannot move."

Exhaling slowly, he raised his gaze to hers. "With what remained of my inheritance, I funded Dr. Griffiths so he could help others as he did me."

Around them, other patrons laughed and ate their ices, and weren't in the midst of their heart breaking. She cleared her throat. "Yes. Clearly, you squandered your inheritance."

Startled dark eyes met hers.

She shifted under his intense stare. "Why do you look at me so?"

"Who are you?" he asked.

"What do you mean? You know who I am."

After another long stare, he shook his head.

Uncertain why he'd asked such a thing, she firmed her shoulders. Ultimately, it didn't matter why. "Who are these persons who believe your inheritance wasted?"

His lips twisted. "My brother."

"Lord Roxwaithe?" she asked, surprised.

He nodded once, sharply.

"Why would he think that?"

"Why wouldn't he think it? He has always thought me useless."

Such bitterness. She wanted to ask him why. Why did his brother think him useless? Why did he allow it? But Stephen's shuttered expression declared louder than a verbal protest he would not answer.

"I have only ever seen my father once, and my mother never." She was more surprised than he that she'd spoken.

She saw again her father behind the desk in Tidswell House's study, his fierce scowl. "My father is away to Ceylon, and returned to England only once upon my mother's death. My mother, she never returned from Italy. She is buried there."

"We are both poorly served by our families."

Her eyes burned and she could not speak. Again, the mundane commotion of the tea shop surrounded them. Murmured voices and the clink of metal on plates.

"We've exceeded our allotted time," he finally said. "Let us collect your maid and be on our way."

She could only nod. Taking the hand he offered, she allowed him to escort her from the table, their half-eaten ices left forlornly behind. Ahead, Delphine spied their movements, abandoning her own ice to make her way to them.

Stephen's gaze drifted past Sera and his expression

changed, becoming heavy lidded. "Lady Seraphina, you've come undone," he murmured.

"I beg your pardon?" The words had barely past her lips before his hand gently cradled hers, turning her palm upwards. His fingers traced a path of the sensitive middle, over the mound of her thumb. Though she wore gloves, she could feel the heat from his fingers, the gentle caress of his skin trailing over hers through the cloth. He drifted over her wrist, and suddenly his fingers met her flesh. She sucked in her breath, and it seemed strangled inside her, her gaze locked on his lowered one as he traced the gap the undone button had made between glove and skin.

"As I said," his voice was low, intimate. "You've come undone."

She watched, breathless, as with a gentle flick he brought the button closed, his fingers lingering a touch too long before he slowly raised his gaze. She was caught by his dark eyes, everything around them fading as she lost herself in him.

"Do you think he was convinced?" he asked, his lips barely moving.

She blinked. "Pardon?"

"Sutton. Do you think he was convinced?"

It was playacting only. It wasn't real.

She pulled her hand from his. "I would say yes. You were persuasive." To say the least of it. Somehow, he had persuaded *her*. More fool she was.

"Good. I presume that is why you brought us here, because you knew he would be here also."

"Of course." She offered a smile, and if it felt garish and wrong, she took comfort in knowing she performed it so often, no one else saw the difference. "Come, we must to the booksellers. We are already late."

A frown touched his brow. "Seraphina…"

"Come, Stephen. We must away." Turning her smile brighter, she took his arm and urged them to leave.

He allowed her this, though his brows were still drawn. He did not question, and they passed the rest of the afternoon looking to all the world like a couple in early courtship.

But she knew it to be false. He had, after all, reminded her.

Chapter Nine

THE VISCOUNTESS QUINN'S ASSEMBLY was the most coveted of events. Always a lavish affair, everyone who was anyone craved an invitation, and this year's ball was no exception. The hallways and ballroom of Quinn House teemed with guests, marvelling at the extravagance and the glamour as the Viscountess outdid herself yet again. Peonies and baby's breath dripped from the buttresses and archways against a backdrop of evergreen sprigs. Tiny candles winked in the foliage, glinting off spun-silver spanning like spider web across the greenery.

In the refreshments room, guests crowded around tables laden with extravagant delicacies: exotic fruits, delicate sandwiches, pastries that melted in one's mouth, while a pyramid of champagne glasses towered over an enormous punch bowl.

Taking a sip of her punch, Sera pretended idleness as she examined the crowd. Ladies Gordon, Hutton and Adams gathered by the four-tiered, elaborately decorated cake, their gazes sweeping the room as they gossiped amongst themselves. Opposite, Lady Gresham stood with her cohort, glaring at the trio even as she surveyed the crowd through her looking glass.

The biggest gossips in London in perfect view of where Sera stood. Everyone knew one attended Viscountess Quinn's assembly to see and be seen, that the gossips in attendance would spread whatever they learned around the Ton by the end of the following day. It was the perfect place to insinuate a connection merely by standing too close to another, to intimate a courtship with nothing more than proximity.

Now all she needed was the man she wanted to be seen with.

Raising her glass, Sera scowled at the liquid. She'd discussed this with Stephen just yesterday as they had toured the museum and she had explicitly stated he was to attend. He'd assured her he would do so, for all he had not quite met her eyes and instead had seemed too enamoured of the display of treasures from Cairo. She'd felt uneasy then and it seemed she had not been wrong to feel so: it had just gone half-ten and he'd not yet arrived.

Across the room, Maria flirted outrageously with Lord Palmer, giggling as she batted him with her fan, while Elizabeth was nowhere to be seen. When she'd first arrived at Quinn House, Sera had been quite content to allow them their solitary pursuits, more concerned with making it so others noticed she was not with her usual companions and taking note of who she *was* with. Now, though, she contemplated rounding them up to attend her and discover just where, exactly, Lord Stephen Farlisle *was*.

Also across the room, Lydia Torrence bent her red-gold head to Violet Crafers blonde one as the Duke of Meacham approached them, an unholy gleam to his eye. That gleam only brightened when Violet Crafers noticed his approach and sent him the most terrific glare.

Sera's gaze touched on a man who glared at *her*. Perfectly coiffed, the sneer twisting the Duke of Sutton's lips ruined his icy perfection. She did not count herself unique, however. He wore the expression often, as if everything and everyone was beneath his condescension. It had been mildly amusing to allow him to court her, to enjoy the adulation his station afforded. It was, however, exceedingly tiresome he could not accept that courtship was now over and further, she had been the one to end it. He deserved to lose the wager with Stephen, and if it helped Stephen's charity, all the better.

Exhaling, she discarded her punch. Everyone was here. Simply everyone. Apart from the man who had *promised* he would be.

"Lady Seraphina?" Clothed in emerald green, Miss Edirisinghe beamed at her. Somehow, the girl had appeared at Sera's side without her notice.

She frowned. The girl's dress was inappropriate. She was young—not more than seventeen, if she had to guess—and bright colours were ill-fitting to debutantes. Sera's own gown was a royal shade of blue but, even though she was unmarried and technically disallowed such shades, she was eight seasons removed from debut. The girl, however, was from Ceylon and perhaps they did things differently in the East.

"I am *so* pleased to finally speak with you," Miss Edirisinghe continued, a slight accent flavouring the words she fairly gushed. "I know we have not formally been introduced, but I have longed to do so for an age."

"Miss Edirisinghe," she greeted.

The girl's smile brightened. "Oh, you know who I am? I am *so* glad. I was hoping this wouldn't be awkward, and now, it won't be. Please, may we take a turn about the room? I am dying to learn *everything* about you."

She could think of no reason to disagree, and she could not yet cut the girl direct. She did not know enough about her, who her connections were, who she, Sera, might offend by offering a slight. It was such a small thing she asked, and Sera had no desire to explain the reason she would refuse some a simple request was she was awaiting the presence of a *man*.

Abruptly, she smiled and took Miss Edirisinghe's arm. "I would be delighted, my dear."

Miss Edirisinghe's smile brightened and they walked through the refreshment room into the entrance hall. The space still teemed with guests, those not dancing or partaking of the copious punch or the tables groaning with food.

Miss Edirisinghe chatted without pause, speaking of her experiences in London and at balls and gatherings. Sera turned a deaf ear to it while she seethed. How was it she had allowed a man to control her actions? She did not wait and fret over the presence of anyone: *She* was the one people waited for.

"The Earl of Roxwaithe," intoned the majordomo.

Sera jerked her gaze around. The Earl of Roxwaithe entered the room, expression unsure as he pulled at the cuffs of his well-tailored evening jacket. His hair was slicked back so one couldn't fairly tell the unfashionable length of it, though his neatly trimmed beard spoke of his unconventional leanings. He was tall and broad and completely different to Stephen in both looks and temperament.

His gaze searched the room and, when he didn't find what he sought, his shoulders slumped. Just as quick, though, he straightened and, with purpose, strode for the ballroom.

Searching for Lydia Torrence, no doubt. Honestly, the drama between them was tiresome, but offered endless opportunities to toy with Lydia.

"Father said I should not seek you out, but I could not help myself." Miss Edirisinghe. The girl continued her chatter, not having noticed Sera's distraction. "How could I come to London and not see you? I told him he had rocks in his head and I would do as I please." Miss Edirsinghe tossed her head and something about the move tugged at Sera's memory. "Of course, I did not say this to him in person, merely in my head. He wouldn't have let me come if he knew I intended to get to know you. My aunt does not know either—my aunt is my chaperone, she has accompanied me on this trip, and she would be horrified if she had discovered my intentions, simply horrified. It does not matter now, though, does it? My plan has worked, we have met, and I am so, so glad."

Sera's gaze slid back toward the entrance. Stephen still wasn't here. Maybe his brother would know where he was.

"I thought to introduce myself as soon as I disembarked from the ship, but my aunt insisted we instead tour the Cotswolds. It has been simply an age, Lady Seraphina, and I have no idea how I constrained myself for so long. How was it I kept myself from seeking out my sister the very *second* I set foot in England?"

Shock jerked Sera's head around.

Miss Edirisinghe continued, joy fairly exploding from her. "He's the most wonderful father, isn't he? It's so kind of you to share him with me. That's what he always says, that his England family shares him with his Ceylon family."

A roaring began in Sera's ears.

"May I call on you? I so want to get to know you. I have so wanted a sister, especially an older one. Mama and our father have plagued me only with brothers, and so I just know we will get along."

Sera couldn't answer. She couldn't have heard that correctly. Her head... She could not think. She nodded, not knowing to what she agreed.

"I shall call on you. It is decided. Oh, I'm so excited! Shall I send a card? Will your secretary answer? Do you have a secretary? My aunt has a lady's maid who handles her correspondence, but I feel sure you are more modern than she." Her smile faltered. "Oh, there is my aunt now. I shall have to return to her side, but I will send you my card. I am so looking forward to it—" She looked around them surreptitiously and whispered, "Sister." With an excited squeal, she bounced off.

Sera stared after her. The roaring in her head drowned out everything. Her father…had another daughter? And not just a daughter, but sons. In Ceylon. He had a whole family in Ceylon. And he spent time with them and loved them and…and…

And he had not told the daughter he had in London.

Something wild and panicked pulled inside her, tearing her insides. She couldn't breathe. She couldn't—

The roar inside her worsened, blades sharpening. She couldn't calm. She needed—

Red-gold hair. A curvaceous figure. Focussed, she set a path. "Lady Lydia, so lovely to see you."

Lydia Torrence turned, her expression filled with dread. "Lady Seraphina."

Arranging her face into a pretty smile, she ignored the blades in her chest. "We did not catch up properly at the Fanning ball. It has been an age since we spoke, why surely before you left for the Continent. Remind me again why there was such a rush for you to depart?"

"No reason," Lydia said.

"Ah. Well, it was peculiar and many commented on it at the time. However, that is now past, is it not, and you have such delicious new gossip. Tell me about the Duke of Meacham. He seems quite taken with you. Though, if I recall correctly, you had forever set your cap for another." This feeling, this churn inside her, it wasn't lessening. Why wasn't it lessening? Desperately, she continued, trying something new, trying something that would wound. "Were you not to wed Lord Roxwaithe? Should we expect an announcement shortly?" The hole inside Sera refused to close. Instead, it pulsed as she watched Lydia swallow.

Holding her chin up, Lydia kept her gaze locked with Seraphina's. It wasn't working. Baiting Lydia wasn't working. Why wasn't it working?

Desperation drove her to continue. "I have been scouring the papers daily awaiting the bans. Do share what is taking so long. Perhaps it is Lord Roxwaithe has not yet proposed? Whatever could be keeping him? Or is it that he just does not want you. Is that it? Did you declare yourself and he refused? He would have done it gently, would he not? Lord Roxwaithe is nothing if not a gentleman."

"Why are you doing this?" Lydia asked, her voice cracking.

Sera froze, uncertainty churning in her gut. Why did she do it? Because it had always worked before. In the past, she had aimed a sharp, honeyed tongue at her target and the pain had lessened, had become something she was able to bear, and it had *always* worked before. Why wasn't it now?

In the end, she smiled thinly and said, "Because, my dear, I don't like you. Do be sure to invite me to the wedding." Tapping her fan lightly against Lydia's arm., she gave another smile as she glided away, somehow keeping the pieces of herself together.

It could have been minutes or it could have been hours as she wandered the ball, smiling pleasantly and making conversation. She must have made sense, as none commented on her distraction, and then suddenly Stephen stood before her, a smile on his full mouth.

"Lady Seraphina. Fancy seeing you here," he said drily.

She couldn't respond. She stared at him, her heart racing, her vision blurring.

His brow creased. "Seraphina?"

"Lord—" She swallowed, wet her lips. "Lord Stephen."

"Are you well?"

"I am—" She wasn't. She wasn't well. She was— "Have you just arrived?"

"I have. I apologise I did not arrive as we agreed. I was delayed. Unavoidably."

She nodded.

His frown deepened. "Sera?"

She made a noise. It might have been an assent.

Still with furrowed brow, he touched her cheek. His fingers came back wet.

She was crying? She didn't cry. She was Seraphina Waller-Mitchell. She made others cry.

"Sera, what is wrong?"

"You shouldn't be touching me. It is inappropriate."

"There is no one to see."

She glanced about them. They were in a cool, dark room. How had that happened? She shook her head. She couldn't remember.

"Sera." His hand cupped her cheek. He was warm. So

warm. "What is wrong?"

She could say cruel things. Cutting things. She could make the concern in his eyes disappear, could make it so he lost all expression and stared at her with none at all, could make it so his pain would make hers disappear.

Instead, she threw herself into him.

His arms came around her hesitantly and she burrowed into him, her hands digging into his back as she pushed her cheek into his chest, wanting his warmth, his comfort. His arms tightened around her, and she felt his lips rub against her forehead, his voice soothing nonsense, and she shook and shook.

Eventually, the shaking stopped. Gentle, soothing hands stroked her back and, closing her eyes, she let herself breathe. "How did we get in here?"

"I followed you. Do you not remember?"

She shook her head, her cheek rubbing against the fabric of his jacket.

"Do you wish to return to the ballroom?"

"Not yet." She took a breath. "Will you stay?"

Chin resting on her head, he nodded. "Are you now well?"

She didn't want to answer. If she answered, she would have to let him go.

"Sera?" His thumb lifted her chin. Dark brown eyes met hers. "Are you now well?"

Reluctantly, she nodded.

He nodded once in return, sharply. Then he pulled her tighter.

He wasn't going to let go. A lump rose in her throat, and she felt like crying again.

"What was all that about?" he asked softly.

She shook her head. She didn't want to think about it.

"Sometimes it's better to talk about it, but you don't have to. You can if you want."

She shook her head again. She couldn't talk of Miss Edirisinghe and her father—she took a shuddering breath.

The corner of his mouth kicked up. "Maybe later, then."

There was the hint of a reddish beard on his jaw and she stroked the line of it. "Your valet did not shave you properly."

He sucked in his breath. "What?" he said, his tone husky.

"Your beard." She followed the line of his jaw with her fingers. It was strong and square and it was definitely— "It is red."

"It is not red. It's a slightly darker blond."

"It's red," she said finally.

Again, his mouth kicked up. "Well, you are clearly recovered."

Suddenly, she became aware of how close they stood to each other, how his arms were still around her. How strong they felt. Wordlessly, she stared up at him.

His expression changed, his eyes darkening. "Sera," he said.

Her gaze drifted to his mouth.

He wet his lips. "Sera."

She shivered.

His head bent to hers even as she lifted to him. Her lips met his. He was soft and full beneath her mouth, and oh so gentle.

She'd been kissed before, often, and she'd always enjoyed it. She wouldn't have done it if she hadn't. But this…this was different. *He* was different. His hand cupped her jaw, his thumb running over her cheek as his fingers traced the skin behind her ear.

His tongue flicked at the seam of her mouth and she opened to him, her fingers tangling in his coat as she brought herself closer to him.

They kissed again and again, and she wanted it to continue, wanted to kiss him until she'd forgotten everything.

But she couldn't.

She ended the kiss, exhaling. He rubbed his mouth against her forehead.

"Is this part of the bet?"

"What?" He pulled back. His mouth was reddened, his lips slightly swollen. From her mouth. From their kiss.

She cleared her throat. "Are you hoping that would assist with the bet?"

His eyes shuttered. "Ah. The bet. Of course."

She had said the wrong thing. He was pulling away from her. "I liked it," she blurted.

Surprise lit his eyes. "Pardon?"

She cursed herself. She never blurted. She was always assured in what she said, what she did. She cleared her throat again. "You kiss quite well."

"*Quite* well?"

She nodded. "Adequately."

"Well. Perhaps we should do it again. You could give me pointers."

"Not tonight. I'm busy."

He laughed, warm and rich and deep.

Warmth filled her. She did love it when she made him laugh. Something told her he had not much laughter in his life.

The back of his fingers brushed her temple, his thumb collecting the last of the wetness on her cheek. "Shall we return to the ballroom?"

Nodding, she closed her eyes as he swept his thumb over her cheek again.

His hand travelled over her jaw, her neck, rested on her shoulder before lifting. When she opened her eyes, he gave her a half-smile and his arm.

Taking his arm, she let him lead her from the room.

Chapter Ten

ACROSS THE HEATH, STEPHEN drove the ball down the field. Face a mask of concentration, his muscles moved under his shirt as his strong thighs hurled him down the pitch, striking the ball to keep it ever before him.

Tongue pressed to her upper teeth, Sera watched him. She had no notion a football match could be so thrilling. Stephen was mesmerising, fluidity and strength and speed. She couldn't tear her gaze from him, his shirt stuck to his chest, in places transparent and displaying the hint of firm golden flesh. His breeches hugged tight to the heavy muscles of his thighs, and she felt hot and faint and she wanted badly to trace the lines of his chest.

They had attended several more societal gatherings—balls, garden parties, musicales—and she had thought no more on Miss Edirisinghe and her revelation. The girl had attempted to call but each time Sera had pretended absence, to the point where Higgins's expression had turned slightly reproving. She didn't want to think on her father and what it meant that he had spent his presence the whole of Miss Edirisinghe's life, while his oldest daughter could count his presence in a number of hours.

The final whistle sounded. Wiping at the corner of her eye, she smiled as a boy locked hands in celebration with Stephen, a wide grin splitting his face. He said something and Stephen responded, running his hand through his damp hair. The move pulled his shirt tight against his bicep, the muscles straining against the fabric.

Sera's mouth went dry.

He finished speaking with the boy, clapping him on the

shoulder, and, spying her, a huge smile lit his face. She told herself the thrill that ran through her was due to the chill in the air, or residual emotion from the game. He started toward her and she watched his progress, lifting her chin as he stopped before her.

"You came," he greeted her.

"I did."

Propping his foot on the fence she leant against, he said, "You had the loftiest expression on your face when I invited you, as if I had insulted you terribly. I did not think you would come."

She sniffed. "Well, you were wrong."

He grinned and she fought the tugging at her own lips. "What did you think?"

"It was...energetic, was it not? Congratulations on your victory." She raised a brow. "At least, I assume that was what all the punching and shoving was about."

"It was indeed. We're five-one for the season. Not bad, if I do say so myself."

She nodded as if she knew of what he spoke.

His grin widened. "You have no idea what I'm talking about, do you?"

Glaring at him, she tossed her head.

He laughed.

A man loped over to them, beaming. "You won!" he shouted excitedly.

Stephen rolled his eyes. "You state the obvious, Ash."

"Two to nil! A triumph! You didn't even bugger it all up!"

"Your faith in me is astounding. Also, you have managed to curse in the presence of a lady."

The man—who Sera now saw was the Earl of Ashburton—blanched. "Apologies, my lady. My excitement ran away from me."

"No need for apologies, Lord Ashburton. The game was rather thrilling."

The earl grinned. "And this fellow here does insist on being annoyingly talented with a football. What is this now, your twentieth year playing?"

"Certainly. If you count when I was eleven and quite average."

"As if you were ever average. As I said, Lady Seraphina,

it is annoying."

She looked between the two. Lord Ashburton still grinned at Stephen, who did not smile but was subtly amused. "So you are talented, Lord Stephen?"

"I am. At…many things." A lazy glint in his eyes.

"Indeed? What, pray tell, are these things of what you speak?"

"Stamina, my lady, and patience. Both are necessary."

"For football?" she said archly.

"Of course. What else, pray tell, could we refer to?"

"I'm sure I don't know, sir."

"I am still here, you know," Ashburton said mildly.

They both looked at him.

Colour high, Sera arranged a smile. "Of course, Lord Ashburton. We merely jest."

"Yes. I can see that."

Stephen lost the wicked glint in his eye. "I better get back. We've got to review the game."

Sera frowned. "Review the game?"

Stephen nodded. "I'll see you both this evening."

"At the Peterson's," Lord Ashburton said.

Stephen nodded again, shortly. Then, he jogged back onto the field to join his teammates.

Sera and Lord Ashburton watched him silently. She had not before had much occasion to converse with Lord Ashburton. Though they attended the same balls and gatherings, their paths did not often cross.

He opened his mouth as if to speak, but then seemed to think better of it. She glanced at him as he again went to speak, and again thought better of it.

"Do you wish to say something, Lord Ashburton?"

Given permission, the words rushed from him. "Lady Seraphina. My conscience will not allow my silence. You know Farlisle toys with you?"

Shoulders tense, concern drew lines into his face. "You may rest easy, Lord Ashburton. I am aware of the wager."

"You know Farlisle means to engage your emotions and then disappoint you?"

"I do."

"And how do you feel about this?"

She smiled viciously. "I feel Sutton is about to lose two hundred pounds."

Visibly relieved, a sunny smile lit his face. "Ah. Good. Good. I told Farlisle it was bad business, but he assured me all will be well." He leant forward conspiratorially. "Sutton deserves whatever's coming."

Amused, she inclined her head. "He does indeed."

"You're good for him, you know."

She glanced at him in surprise. "Pardon?"

"You make him smile. Farlisle. He doesn't smile much, not since Harbor passed. Soccer and you, that seems to be the total of it."

She didn't know what to say.

The corner of Lord Ashburton's mouth kicked up. "It's good," he assured. "He should smile more. He can't go through life being so grim all the time."

She looked down at her hands. She didn't know what to think.

"Will you be here Saturday next, Lady Seraphina? Perhaps we can hurl insults at Farlisle together."

Would she attend next Saturday? It was not a requirement of her plan to win the wager. There was no one to see them, bar Lord Ashburton. No one to comment on their supposed courtship, to report back their closeness to the Duke of Sutton.

On the field, Stephen glanced over, and his smile warmed her.

Softly, she said, "I will."

Chapter Eleven

A WOMAN IN AN orange dress pretended badly she wasn't staring at their box.

Stephen returned her stare however, as he was higher up and concealed by shadow, he would wager he was doing a much better job of hiding his interest. She was young, perhaps not much more than seventeen, and the rich brown of her skin and her cloud of black hair suggested she hailed from a place far more intriguing than England.

The woman by her side, also of the same colouring, snapped her fan open and spoke in a clear rebuke. No doubt she deemed the girl's behaviour unladylike, judging by the very proper way she held herself. The girl merely grinned, her exuberance obvious even from this vantage, but she turned her gaze from the box.

Exhaling, Stephen turned his own gaze from her. The intermission between performances seemed to drag on more each time he attended the theatre, and he could feel himself becoming antsy, the muscles in his legs twitching. He found it difficult to sit still at the best of times, let alone when his brain was unoccupied, however he couldn't pass up the offer from Ash to occupy his box while his friend was out of town, especially as it fitted in with Sera's schedule.

She sat straight-backed in her chair beside him now, her profile in relief. Every so often, she would glance at the woman in the orange dress. Then she'd glance at Oliver's box. Then stare straight ahead.

Four boxes down, Oliver sat with Lydia Torrence. It appeared they were friends again, but his brother gazed upon her like she was the answer to every question. Oliver hadn't noticed him, and Stephen intended to keep it that way.

His gaze drifted to his brother and Lydia Torrence. "Who do you study?"

Sera started. "I beg your pardon?" she asked haughtily.

The corner of his mouth twitched. She always pretended arrogance when she didn't know how else to react. "My brother or Lady Lydia. Who do you study?"

The faintest blush lit her cheeks, but she raised her chin and glared. "Neither," she said, her tone implying he was insolent for even asking.

At her response, he couldn't help his grin.

"Don't smirk. It's unbecoming."

He didn't reply, but he did continue to smirk.

Breath exploding, she crossed her hands in her lap, her concession to annoyance, he supposed. "You are maddening, you realise."

"I do." She sniffed, and his grin widened. He didn't know when it happened, but he loved spending time with her.

She'd come to several of his football practices and matches since the first, and he'd squired her about town as per their agreement, but he found himself looking forward to the next time he would see her, and when they were together, he enjoyed every moment. They spoke of everything and nothing, and he found her company the one he wanted most.

Sera's gaze drifted again to the girl in the orange gown. Her imperiousness died, something haunted instead painting her expression.

Frowning, he followed her gaze. He could see nothing to prompt such a reaction, merely the girl in the orange gown. "What is wrong?"

"Hmm?" she said without turning to him.

"There is something wrong. What is it?"

"Nothing is wrong."

His frown deepened. He watched her watch the girl and waited.

"What?" she finally asked.

"Nothing. Because apparently nothing is wrong." Reaching out, he rubbed his thumb over the top of the gloved hand in her lap.

Startled grey eyes met his. "What are you doing?"

Giving her a lazy smile, he traced her knuckles. "Getting

your attention."

Her breath caught, and then she scowled. "Well, now you have it, and the attention of every gossip hungry matron of the Ton," she said tartly. "You know what they will say."

"No, I don't."

Colour high, she shot him a look filled with annoyance. She couldn't disguise, though, the rapid rise and fall of her breasts. Fascinated, he dragged his thumb over the delicate veins on the back of her hand and she stifled a gasp. "They will comment on your action, and it will become more than it is, and then we shall have to marry."

Heart thundering, he shifted his legs, hiding his rapidly hardening cock. "All because I touched your hand?"

"Marriages have been started with much less," she said darkly.

What was it about that tone that arrowed straight to his cock? Leaning forward, he took her hand between his. "Oh, no. It looks like we are doomed."

"Stephen," she hissed, trying to tug away.

He refused to let go. "What if I do this?" He flicked open the first button nearest her wrist.

"Wh-what are you doing?" She licked her lips.

Christ, her tongue. He wanted it. Ignoring her, he caressed the second button open.

Her breath caught.

He couldn't tear his gaze from the small patch of skin he was revealing. Her pulse fluttered beneath delicate flesh, all soft and creamy. He wondered if it was as delicious as it looked.

Mesmerised, he made to bring her wrist to his lips.

"Stephen," she said, her voice husky. Lifting his gaze to hers, darkened grey eyes captured his, and he almost tugged her forward, almost forgot they weren't alone.

"Stephen," she said again.

Abruptly, the sounds of the theatre intruded. He let her tug her hand from his grasp and he willed his body to calm. Clearing his throat, he forced himself to recall what they were discussing. "There is something wrong, Sera. You keep staring at that girl in the orange dress."

Colour high, she froze in the middle of buttoning her glove. "No, I'm not."

He didn't deign to respond to such a patently false statement.

Closing her eyes briefly, she conceded, "You are right. I was staring."

"Why?"

"I—" Swallowing, she stared down at her gown, her fingers twisting the fabric.

"Sera?" he queried gently.

"Miss Edirisinghe told me— She said—" Slowly, she exhaled. "She is my sister."

Shock stole his tongue.

With a bitter smile, she continued, "My father, it seems, has another family."

He didn't know what to say. She continued to stare at her gown, her fingers twisting and twisting.

"You didn't know?" he asked carefully.

She laughed harshly. "Of course not. Why would my father tell me anything? He never has before. I've seen him once in all my life, when he came to London to administer my mother's estate and even then, I spent less than ten minutes in his company. I attempted to see him again, did you know that? I went to Paris, because he said in his quarterly letter he would be in Paris, so I order a new wardrobe and arranged passage. I was there a month—a whole month—before I realised he would not come. I was there a total of five months and never did he arrive. In his next quarterly letter, he did not even mention why he had not travelled to Paris. I am never his concern." She wiped angrily at her wet cheeks.

He did not know what to say. He rubbed at his chest, wishing he had the words. "What do you want to do?" he finally asked.

"I don't know what to do, Stephen. Miss Edirisinghe wants to get to know me. She wants to call on me, and spend time with me, and she wants us to be sisters. But she's known of me her whole life. I had no idea my father had remarried, that he'd made another family, that he'd…he'd made me a sister. He has…he…he *abandoned* me, Stephen. I don't know what to do." She looked at him, her eyes wet. "What should I do?"

Nothing good would come of this. He couldn't tell her what to do. "I cannot speak for you, Sera."

"But I want to know. I want to know what you would do. What you think *I* should do."

She looked at him as if his opinion were worthy. "Perhaps…you should embrace her." He worked his jaw. Christ.

He didn't want to say the wrong thing. "I have lost a brother. It is...I would give anything to have him back."

She wet her lips. "But you are at odds with your other brother."

Perhaps, but they were not talking of him. "Are you at odds with Miss Edirisinghe?"

"I— Only in the respect I had no idea of her existence and...it seems my father cares for her. Greatly."

"That is his failing, Sera."

An incredulous breath burst from her.

Christ, why didn't he have the words? "It is his failing he doesn't... That he does not see how extraordinary you are. Clearly, your sister realises you are an exceptional human and she would be better off knowing you, having you in her life. Do not punish her for your father's lack."

For the longest time, she stared at him. "He isn't a good father."

He shook his head.

Her gaze drifted to Miss Edirisinghe. "At least, he isn't a good father to me."

"No."

She nodded, and without another word she took his hand between hers, brought them to her lap and looked out to the stage.

He studied her profile. Her cheeks were pale, her chin held high, but her fingers gripped his tight. Silently, he turned his attention to the stage as well.

They sat thus for the rest of the play.

Chapter Twelve

WHISKY GLASS PROPPED ON the arm of the leather chair, Stephen watched patrons of the 1810 Club mill about him. One half of the floor was dedicated to gambling and ladies and gentlemen both enjoyed that entertainment, wagering sums that would keep his charities in funds for years. Close around him, patrons enjoyed as he did the outstanding selection of alcohols however most paired theirs with conversation and perhaps the excellent foodstuffs from the kitchen.

What was Sera doing now? She'd said she had a dinner to attend at an acquaintance's and, as he wasn't invited, he could not join her. He'd been at odds, unsure how to spend his evening, and so he found himself here, contemplating whisky and thinking of her.

She had been distressed at the theatre. He couldn't even comprehend what it must be like discovering a sister—a whole other family, really. She'd said Miss Edirisinghe had mentioned brothers in addition to herself, and he cursed Sera's father for a bastard for never telling his oldest daughter of their existence. It would have taken less than nothing to send a letter—although that also would have been a bastard way to inform one's child of the existence of siblings. Strange also Miss Edirisinghe did not refer to herself as Miss Waller-Mitchell—or even Lady Charuni Waller-Mitchell. Perhaps things were done differently in Ceylon...or perhaps she suspected Sera knew nothing of her existence and sought to be kind.

A pain shot through his hand, and he relaxed his fist. It had tightened without his knowledge, his anger at Sera's father finding expression. Would that the man were before him so he could express his fury.

He sighed. What would that accomplish? Sera would still be upset, and would most likely not cheered if Stephen punched the lights out of her father. Better the man remained in Ceylon so his resolve to leave the man be was never tested.

"Farlisle. Always a pleasure." The Duke of Sutton lowered himself into the chair opposite, his usual sardonic smirk firmly in place.

Wonderful. Thoughts of one bastard had resulted in the appearance of another, but Sera would not be mad if he broke Sutton's face. "Sutton," he said shortly.

"I can see you are delighted by my appearance, Farlisle. Truly, try to control your gushing."

There was little point in responding and so, he didn't.

A smile playing about his mouth, Sutton raised a brow. "How goes our bet?"

That required a response. He supposed. "Fine."

Sutton laughed, a quietly malicious sound. "Your effusiveness knows no bounds."

"Sutton, why are you here?" He had no care to spend any more time than he had to in Sutton's company, and he knew the duke felt the same. They tolerated each other at the meets with the other owners of the 1810 Club, but apart from the bet, they both were quite happy to avoid each other.

"I am here because your lady led me here."

Sera? Sera was here? "What?"

"Lady Seraphina has deigned to patron our establishment. Rather risqué of her, but then she has always been a wicked sort."

Sutton's smirk really was intensely annoying. "Did you discover this in the brief period you courted her?"

He took great satisfaction in the way that bloody smirk slipped. "I think this will be one of the few times I will enjoy losing a bet."

"What makes you believe I shall win?"

Sutton nodded at the room behind Stephen. "Because she is here. Lady Seraphina appears to have followed you with little care for who recognises her. Well done, man. Well done indeed."

Turning, he followed Sutton's gaze. Sera had indeed entered the 1810 Club, her identity barely disguised by the lace mask she wore. She stood with Viscount Harcourt and two women similarly disguised, most likely the viscount's sister,

Lady Elizabeth, and Miss Maria Spencer.

The corner of his mouth kicked up, and he saw the moment she saw him. Her luscious mouth curled into a wicked smile and she arched her brow, daring him to come to her.

Bloody hell, she was bold. Daring, and mischievous, and arch, and he wanted to go to her and crush that wicked, wicked smile with his mouth.

"You seemed to have tempted her to court ruin, Farlisle," Sutton said. "Perhaps I should resign myself the loss of the two hundred pounds."

"You do that," he said, only half-listening to what Sutton had said. Without another word, he rose from his seat and left Sutton behind.

Sera watched him as he approached, her cat's eyes dark and mysterious behind the lace. He let his gaze trail over her and beyond, pretending intense interest in the wall behind her. The corner of her mouth tilted up as she cocked her head, her gaze trained upon him.

Passing her by, he met her eyes for half a second. An invitation.

Her throat moved as she swallowed, her chest rising and falling with each breath.

Making his way from the main room, he could feel her eyes on him as he entered the hallway, could feel the exact moment she decided to follow him. He entered the first billiards room he knew to be empty. Turning, he leant against the billiards table and waited.

In a swirl she entered the room, head proud, shoulders back. Her gown was a deep blue, matched by the lace of her mask, and her dark hair was arranged in complicated swirls.

He couldn't wait to disorder them.

Arms crossed over his chest, he said, "What do you here, my lady?"

That half-smirk returned. The one he wanted to trace with his tongue. "Whatever do you mean, sir?"

"You've come to a wicked place, full of wicked men. Have you no care for your reputation?"

"Don't you know, sir? Wickedness *is* my reputation." That coquettish smile curled her lips further. "Are you not going to reprimand me?"

"Why would I do that?"

A crease appeared between her brows. "Most would."

He studied her. "It is not for me to say. You are an adult woman, past her majority and the head of a household. You have a brain and, it is obvious, you know quite well how to use it."

Her gaze flicked away. "Most would not think so."

He shrugged. "Most people are fools."

Shuddering through a breath, she turned back to him, her eyes holding him captive. "You are a rare man, Stephen Farlisle," she said softly.

Shifting his stance, he shrugged again. He had only spoken the truth, and the churn of emotion her soft words stirred within him had no place in this game they currently played.

With another breath, she squared he shoulders and, circling the table, trailed her fingers over the baize covering the bolster. Before his eyes, she recovered herself, becoming wickedness personified once more. But he knew, beneath the wickedness, she was Sera.

Games, however, were eminently amusing, and he was more than willing to partake. "Do you play?"

Fingers caressing the baize, she cocked her head. "Play?"

He couldn't drag his gaze from her fingers, gently stroking the pile one way, then back. Over and over. He thought of all the places those fingers could dance over, the feel of that light teasing touch on his flesh.

"Billiards." The word was a garbled mess.

"No." She swished around the end of the table, making sure her skirts flared to display her ankles. He, of course, noticed, precisely as she'd intended. "Show me?"

Without a word, he strode for the rack adhered to the wall and dislodged a cue, one he judged well-suited to her height. Not, he knew, that she had any interest in using it. This was all part of the game. "What is this?"

She looked at the cue. Then she looked at him. "A stick."

Christ. A single word should not make him shudder. "It is a cue. This is what you hit the ball with." Making his way to her, he took her hand and wrapped it around the cue. "Feel the weight of it," he murmured.

Wide eyes held his. Nervously, her tongue darted out to wet her lips.

He stifled a groan. His cock, already aching, hardened further. Forcing himself to focus, he slid her hand along the cue. "Feel how smooth it is. How strong. Absorb the length of it, the width."

Her tongue wet the corner of her upper lip. "Are you sure we are speaking of the cue?"

A smile tugged at his own mouth. "Of course. What else would we speak of?" Taking her other hand, he positioned it on the cue. "Now, we bring it to the table." Turning her, he positioned the cue in her grip, his chest scraping her back as he stood behind her. "Hold it in your hand, like so." He slid his hand over hers, positioning her fingers.

Her back pressed against his chest as she drew breath, her skirts curling around his legs. Bracing his hands against the table, he caged her within his arms as he battled with himself to keep this ostensibly about teaching her billiards when what he really wanted was to haul her into his arms. "Sera," he said thickly.

She bowed her head, the nape of her neck vulnerable. "Yes?" she replied breathlessly.

Loose strands of hair decorated the bared nape of her neck. He stared at the soft-looking skin, wanting to know its taste. "Do you know what happens to women who follow men into abandoned rooms?"

Dropping the cue, she turned in the circle of his arms, her mouth a whisper from his. "What happens to them, Stephen?"

"I—" He couldn't think. He could only stare at her mouth, at the lips slightly reddened with cosmetics and wet from the sweep of her tongue.

"Is it the same thing that happens to the wicked men who lure them?" Her hands curled around his forearms as she leant closer. "Do they discover how the other tastes?" Her eyes drifted to his mouth. "Can I kiss you?"

Beguiled, he nodded, and then she took his mouth with her kiss.

She kissed him aggressively, with determination, and Christ he loved it. He loved her boldness, her determination. He loved her wickedness, how she'd dared to come to a gambling hell knowing all the consequences and dismissing them. He loved her playfulness, and her pain, and that she controlled the kiss. He let her play with him, her sweet mouth teasing his, making him desperate, making him hard. He leant into her and her hands gripped his hair, holding him still for her pleasure.

And he loved it.

Chapter Thirteen

STRONG ARMS BRACKETED HER as soft lips moulded to the demands of her own. Tangling her fingers in his soft hair, Sera pulled Stephen closer, his hard chest scraping the tips of her aching breasts. At his groan, a thread of triumph twined through the thrill of pleasure, but he stayed motionless against her, the faintest sliver of air between them as he held himself from her. She wanted more. She wanted to drive him wild. She wanted him to break. She wanted to feel the force of his passion, for him to grab her and take her and show her he wanted her as much as she wanted him.

She licked at his upper lip.

He stiffened, lurching fiercely into her a moment but he restrained himself, holding from her so they were only joined by her hands in his hair and her mouth on his. Sweet, gentle, and a tease. She made a sound a back of her throat, and she felt the shape of his wicked smile against her mouth. He knew she wanted more, and she knew he was keeping it from her.

Well. She couldn't have that.

She slid her fingers over his scalp, his neck, tracing his shoulders as she brushed her lips over his again and again. He grunted, but he didn't break, his breath sweet against her tongue as she traced the seam of his lips, the corners of his mouth. Her heart throbbed within her, and the determination to make him lose himself. Curling her hands around his forearms, she pressed herself against him and licked his lips.

With that, she broke him.

He hadn't moved, but somehow he had wrest control, his mouth open against hers and his tongue demanding. She moaned as he stole into her mouth, and she pressed herself closer, her breasts flattening against the lean muscles of his chest.

Pulling his mouth from hers, he ran his thumb over her bottom lip slowly and he murmured, "You shouldn't tempt me."

A thrill raced through her. "Nor should you tempt me."

The corner of his mouth lifted. "Are we playing that game?"

She hadn't thought of it as such. This was…real to her. Breath caught in her chest, she whispered, "Is this a game, Stephen?"

His smile faded as his gaze searched hers. Then he said softly, "No."

A sigh escaped her, and she closed her eyes as his fingers traced the lines of his face: the sweep of her brow, the curve of her cheek, the shape of her jaw. A gentle tug and he removed the mask, his hand trailing down her neck to flatten over the exposed flesh above her bodice, warm and heavy. Her breath came faster, and faster still, and she met his gaze, his eyes burning into hers.

Straightening, he lifted her, seating her on the edge of the billiard table. He slid his hands up her calves, dragging her skirts with them. Gaze holding hers, he moved between her legs, his hips pushing her wider as he trailed his fingers over the outside of her thighs. Her breath caught as she felt him against her, hard and hot. His touch drifted to delicate skin of her inner thighs and then brushed the curls of her mound. Her legs jerked and she bit her lip, her entire body flushing with heat. She had allowed no one this, but she would allow him. She would allow him anything. She wanted to steal this time with him, this moment when they were wicked.

His fingers stilled. She whimpered, but he didn't move, fierce gaze locked on hers and his fingers so close to where she ached. He was asking something of her, but she couldn't think. He had stopped because…he had stopped… Permission. He wanted her permission. He wanted to know she wanted this.

In answer, she pushed herself into his touch.

Hunger flared in his eyes and his fingers parted her, finding her wet and swollen and aching. She moaned, her legs tightening on his hips as he dragged his touch through her folds. His lips brushed her ear as she panted against the bared skin of his throat, his flesh hot against her mouth.

"So wet for me, Sera," he crooned. "I've barely touched you and you're already flowing."

She moaned, her fingers digging into the baize as he teased her opening, spreading her wetness to caress the spot her pleasure centred. His finger circled her before dipping inside.

A cry escaped her, her body rigid, and he growled, his tongue tracing the cord of her neck. "You're so soft, Sera. Soft and hot and sweet. I wonder if you'll taste like that."

Brushing his lips over her mouth, he sank to his knees. He kissed her stomach through the fabric of her dress, his hands curling around her thighs to drag her closer to the edge.

Her startled gaze flew to his.

His eyes burned into hers. "Can I kiss you?"

In a daze, she nodded.

Lust flared in his expression, then he lowered his gaze. Holding her wide, he stared at her.

Heat flushed her cheeks and her legs twitched, trying to close.

"So beautiful." Lowering his head, his lips brushed her inner thigh and then he put his mouth upon her.

It was too much. This was too much. She couldn't—She didn't— A scream built inside as his mouth devoured her, his tongue swirling around that nub of flesh that drove her insane with pleasure. She squirmed and bucked, and he growled against her before he thrust his tongue inside her.

Stifling her scream, she gripped his hair with her hands. His fingers dug into her hips as he thrust again and again. Pleasure ripped through her, her body bowing with the force of it, and she lost herself to the storm.

Gasping, she came back to herself, her body twitching with aftershocks. He rose and took her mouth fiercely, and she tasted herself and him, and she'd never tasted anything sweeter.

Belatedly, she realised he was rigid against her, throbbing against her thigh. "What about you?" she managed, her voice hoarse.

In answer, he kissed her again, but she wouldn't be deterred. He had just given her the most sublime pleasure and she wanted the same for him. "Stephen, what about—"

"It's not a game, Sera, and it's not necessary."

But she wanted to give him what he had given her. "But—"

"This was for you." He pulled back, smoothing her skirts over her legs, and she felt cold without his heat against her. He braced himself over her a moment, his breath harsh. Finally, he gave her a crooked smile. "We should return you to your friends. They will be wondering where you are."

"They know I am with you."

"All the more reason we should go. I will remain here a while after you go. I am...not decent." He handed her the lace mask. She hadn't even realised he had it. She blushed as she remembered why she had been so distracted. "You should go. There is still your reputation."

"No one will dare comment," she replied, fixing the mask in place. She stilled. "Perhaps they should. There is, after all, your wager."

He shrugged. "Sutton spoke to me earlier. He is content. There is no need to tempt gossip."

A twinge of hurt slid through her. She shook herself. *Don't be ridiculous, Sera.* Of course they should not tempt fate. He had no wish to wed her, as she had no wish to wed him. This was for the wager only and she...well, eventually she would think of something that would irritate Lydia Torrence. They had an agreement. What had just happened was a...a... pleasant bonus. A game. Nothing irrevocable had occurred and she had experience great pleasure. There was nothing more to be said.

Affixing a saucy grin, she trailed her finger over his arm. "I thank you for a most pleasant diversion, sir."

His lips twitched. "A pleasure, my lady."

"Perhaps, sometime soon, we could repeat the experience...or perhaps even expand upon it."

Heat flared in his dark eyes. "Perhaps."

With another grin, she sauntered from the room, and she told herself that flash of hurt had been a momentary lapse of reason and nothing more.

Chapter Fourteen

ANTICIPATION PRICKING HIS SKIN, Stephen handed his hat and gloves to Sera's butler. The butler's expression remained impassive, but disapproval fairly radiated from him.

Stephen tipped his chin. So it was not normal hours a gentleman visited a lady, but he was impatient to see Sera and he wouldn't allow a servant to make him ashamed for his eagerness.

"Who may I say is calling, sir?" the butler queried.

"Lord Stephen Farlisle. Brother to the Earl of Roxwaithe," he added. He disliked invoking his brother's name, but if it would get the butler to announce him that much quicker, he would shout it to kingdom come.

"Very good, my lord. Follow me."

The butler led him through the entrance hall and into a receiving room. "Please wait here, my lord. I will see if Lady Seraphina is at home to visitors."

Lacing his hands behind his back, he paced the room, unable to stand still when the desire to see Sera thrummed in his veins. The door flung open and, with a red face and disordered hair, Sera flew through. She almost skidded to a stop, her cheeks pinkening further. The butler trailed behind her, his expression slightly disapproving.

"Good morning, Lord Stephen," she greeted, her hand smoothing over her hair as if she had just realised it was disordered.

The shape of his grin felt loony. "Lady Seraphina."

"It is so lovely you have come to call. Would you like to take tea?"

Amused by the formality, he replied gravely, "I would."

"Higgins, tea. And Mrs Travers's gingernuts, please."

"Of course, my lady." The butler shot Stephen a look before departing, closing the door behind him. The butler was protective of Sera, and had quite clearly warned Stephen in the subtle way the best servants could. Stephen could hardly fault him for that.

They stood awkwardly for a moment. "Please, sit," she said belatedly, arranging herself on one of the chaises.

He lowered himself beside her. Startled, she glanced at him in query but he only lay his arm on the back of the chaise, his fingers almost brushing her shoulder. Perhaps it was not proper, but he could think of no good reason not to sit beside her when they were alone.

"It is fine weather we are having," she finally said.

His lips twitched. "Really? Again with this?"

"I don't know what to say," she burst out. "After…last night…" Her cheeks blushed a fiery red.

Memory wound around him and his breath grew short as his cock grew hard. Subtly, he shifted his seat. Maybe it wasn't the wisest course of conversation. "Perhaps we should talk of our plan."

She shot him a grateful look. "Yes, our plan. We have another ball to go to this evening."

"Another? Why are there so many balls? The season is done."

She lifted a shoulder. "And yet, the Ton remains in London and we *must* have our amusements."

Again, his lips twitched. "Yes. We must, mustn't we."

She returned his smile. "Now, what was so urgent you came at such an early hour?"

"Nothing."

Her brows drew. "Nothing? So why are you here?"

Heat burned his cheeks. "I, ah, wanted to see you?"

Her expression softened. "When Higgins said you were here, I did not wait for my maid to complete my hair," she confessed.

He tugged one of the tumbled curls. "I can see that."

Her grey eyes darkened. "Stephen."

He cleared his throat. "Yes?"

"I think I should like to do something for you now."

And just like that, his aching cock hardened fully. Heart

racing, he licked his lips. "Would you, now?"

Pushing at his shoulders, she pulled up her skirts to straddle him. Leaning forward, her luscious mouth brushed his ear. "We shall have to be quick. The tea comes."

Bloody hell, and if she moved even slightly, so would he. Where was his bloody control? Oh that's right, she'd bloody destroyed it when she'd said she wanted to do something for him. "Sera, you don't have to—"

She swallowed his feeble protest with her mouth, her tongue tangling with his. Hand trailing down his chest, she brushed her fingers over his throbbing cock. Cupping him through his breeches, she gave him a wicked smile. "So hard for me, Stephen."

He managed a laugh at her arch comment. "Always."

Her eyes flickered. "Truly?"

Christ, yes. Always. For her. Barely able to speak, he nodded.

Sliding down, she knelt between his wide-spread knees, her fingers plucking at the buttons of his breeches. She'd barely brushed him before he closed his hands over hers. "Sera, you really don't—"

She scowled. "Stephen, stop it. I want this. I want you. Now lie back, be quiet, and enjoy what I'm doing to you."

Knowing it would win him no favour if he told her how adorable she looked while cross, he did as she bade. "Yes, my lady."

She ran her hand up and down, her fascinated gaze following her movements. He gritted his teeth, reciting what he could remember of the charitable charter to stop himself from coming. A bead of wetness formed at his head and her thumb swept it away, massaging it into his skin.

At his strangled groan, her gaze flew to his. "Am I doing this right?"

Any more right and he'd be coming over her hand. "Yes," he managed.

Her eyes dropped to his cock. "What does it taste like?"

A vivid image of her lips wrapped around him almost made him spill. "Christ Jesus."

"I think I shall find out," she said, and took him into her mouth.

His fingers dug into the chaise, his hips bucking. Her mouth was hot and wet and it took everything inside him not to come in her mouth and shock the life out of her. Her tongue worried the ridge of his cockhead, and the pleasure just about sent him blind. Her hand wrapped around his base, lifting him up so she could run her tongue over him.

"What do you like?" she asked.

"The head," he managed. "Suck the head and wrap your hand around me. Like this." He showed her and she took to it with enthusiasm, driving him insane with hot, wet heaven.

"Sera, I'm going to— You've got to stop," he gasped.

Ignoring him, she sank him further into her, her grip tightening.

"You've got to— Sera, stop,"

She pulled off with a wet pop, her brows drawn. Wrapping his hand around hers, he pumped them both until the orgasm ripped from him, his come mostly captured by his handkerchief.

Taking great gulps of air, his chest heaved as Sera nestled beside him, staring at her hand. "I haven't done that before."

He grunted, unable to say anything.

"It was rather fun. We should definitely do it again."

Flinging an arm over his eyes, he groaned. Christ. She was going to kill him. "Did I get it all?"

"Oh yes. My hand is fine."

Tidying himself, he tucked his cock away and did up his breeches. "So do you count us even?"

"Not in the slightest. I feel we should both do that again. Often." She smiled slyly.

"Not now. The tea is coming."

"Ah yes, the tea." Her fingers wandered down his chest.

Plucking them from him, he stood and removed himself to the chair opposite. "You're dangerous," he said darkly.

Her smile turned smug.

The door opened. They both started, and Stephen thanked God the maid hadn't been five minutes earlier. "Tea, my lady."

Colour high, Sera sat ramrod straight. "Thank you, Veronica."

The maid set out the tea and biscuits and, if she noticed anything odd about their behaviour, she made no comment on it.

Once she'd left, Sera lifted the teapot. "How do you take it?"

He couldn't help himself. He laughed.

She scowled. "What?"

"Nothing. It's just..." He shook his head. "We are pretending this is a normal morning, a normal visit, and you didn't just bring me off on the chaise upon which you sit."

"Bring you off? Is that what it's called?"

"Among other things." He watched her pour the tea, her colour still high. "Sera?"

"Yes?"

"I like you."

The teapot stilled. "You do?" she asked, her gaze on the cup.

Smile tilting the corner of his mouth, he nodded. She looked flustered, and clearly didn't know what to say. "If we didn't have the bet, would you ...that is..." Christ, his collar felt too tight.

Looking up, wide grey eyes locked on his. "Would I..."

"Would you be amenable to..." He cleared his throat. "Perhaps the wager doesn't have to be the end of things."

"Oh?"

"Perhaps we could continue."

"Perhaps."

"And perhaps we could..."

"Yes?"

"It could be a courtship. A real one. If you wanted." Christ, it was hot in here. Was it hot in here?

Biting her lip, her gaze searched his. "Do you want?"

"I—do."

"Well. I do, too."

"Good."

"Good."

They stared at each other.

Finally, cheeks pink, she stood to bring him the tea. Watching her every step, he took the cup from her and carefully set it on the low table before them. Then, he caught her wrist and tugged. She fell into his lap with a gasp as he curved his arm around her back, settling her against him.

Raising a brow, she said archly, "I thought you didn't want me near you. Your words, I believe, indicated I was dangerous."

He couldn't stop his grin. "I got lonely."

She snuggled in to him, her hand stroking his chest. He played with her hair. Time slipped by, the clock on the mantle keeping it but neither of them noticing.

"I don't want to go," he finally confessed.

She laced her fingers in his. "Then don't."

"I have to go to my brother's."

Attention still on his fingers, her brow creased. "Why?"

"We need funds. I must pretend to once again be the careless, wastrel spendthrift."

She pulled back, his arm dropping to loosely hold her waist. Her gaze searched him and he sat still beneath it, knowing he could only do so because it was her. "It can wait, though?"

Of course. Of course it could. Hauling her back into his arms, he rested his chin on her head as her hands burrowed between his jacket and waistcoat.

It could wait.

Chapter Fifteen

HEAT HUNG HEAVY OVER the ballroom, the air humid and pregnant with the promise of a summer storm. Servants wielding large palm-shaped fans made of wicker and ostrich feathers did their best to move the still air through the ballroom and usher in the hint of coolness from the wide-flung balcony doors, but their efforts amounted to little.

Fanning herself, Sera looked out over the ballroom. The press of bodies made the heat even more oppressive, and guests were beginning to succumb. A lady swooned, while the gentleman she intended to catch her barely did so in time, his expression dazed. Chatter was listless, and those dancing lacked enthusiasm.

She had no care for others, though. Not when, from across the ballroom, Stephen watched her.

Leaning against the ballroom's wall, he crossed his arms over his chest, his focus wholly upon her. He didn't pretend disinterest or tease, didn't look at another woman in an attempt to make her jealous. No, Stephen levelled his gaze upon her and let her know she held all of his attention.

A bead of perspiration slid between her breasts. He held her attention, too. So easily. Sweat sheened his cheekbones, causing skin tanned from countless hours playing football to glow golden. An image of him flashed across her, of him in shirtsleeves that clung to his leanly muscled frame, his cuffs pushed back to reveal strong forearms, and the graceful prowl of his body as he came to her. Another image replaced the first, this time his jacket and shirt disordered by her hands, his throat arched and his body bowed as he yielded to the pleasure she gave him.

Mouth abruptly dry, she parted her lips as pressure pushed low in her abdomen, heavy and empty. How did he do this to her from across a ballroom? Pushing off the wall, he started towards her. Her breath caught, her heart a mad thump in her chest.

Reaching her, he took her hand, bending low. "Lady Seraphina," he murmured, his lips brushing her fingers.

His touch burned as if gloves didn't separate her skin from his. "Lord Stephen," she managed.

He rose, his dark eyes smouldering. "I find I require refreshment."

Her brain felt thick. "You do?"

He nodded, his tongue slicking the flesh of his plush bottom lip. She almost moaned.

"I shall no doubt pass by the orangery, in my search for refreshment."

Belatedly, she realised what he was about. Excitement began a mad thrum. "Indeed. I find I require a bit of fresh air. The heat." She waved generally.

"Yes. I hope we both achieve our desire."

Oh, wicked man. Wicked, wicked man.

He bowed. "Lady Seraphina."

"My lord," she murmured. He bowed again and, with that slight, sly smile she loved, he disappeared into the crowd.

She waited a moment, then another, and then she followed.

The sounds of the ball faded as she made her way down the hallway. A gaggle of ladies passed her, their excited voices fading as they disappeared in the opposite direction. Shadows deepened, pale moonlight offering weak illumination as it spilled from the open corridor doors.

Sera stopped. She was certain she should have reached the orangery by now. Perhaps she had made a wrong turn. Starting back the way she came, she opened a door that had to be the orangery.

The air held a different humidity here, one of trees and shrubs rather than too many bodies, and the faint moonlight painted the orangery to various shades of grey. Outside, lightning crashed. Thunder followed slowly, the storm still some distance from reaching them. Rain had yet to fall, and the air grew thicker.

Another flash of lightning. The orangery lit up, exotic palms throwing strange patterns on the wall. And there, in the middle of the greenery, stood Lydia Torrence and the Earl of Roxwaithe in torrid embrace.

Sera immediately dropped to a crouch, concealing herself behind a potted shrub. They hadn't noticed her, though, wholly immersed in each other, but then, the earl gently pushed Lydia from him. They whispered to each other, and then the earl glanced her way.

Sera's heart stopped.

Lydia said something, and the earl's attention returned to her. Quietly as she could, Sera retreated to the entrance. The door handle turned silently in her hand, and she slipped out.

In the hallway, she placed a hand over her frantic heart. Now that she was in no danger of being seen, she started to think. She had caught Lydia and the earl. If it was made known, there would be scandal. They were not affianced. They weren't even courting. Though everyone knew of Lydia's passion, few knew the earl returned it. He insisted she was too young, and tongues would wag about that very insistence. The damage done to both could be irreparable until they finally succumbed to the inevitable and wed. It was what Lydia wanted, and the earl would have come around to it eventually. Finally, she could ruin Lydia, but...did she want to?

A garish grin stretched her mouth. Of course she did. Of course, and...

It hit her, like the lightning that flashed outside. She could use this. They could use this. She and Stephen. He'd said he needed funds, and surely his brother would pay to keep this information quiet. It had to be done delicately, but it could be done.

"Sera?" Stephen approached, his eyes alight, his lips curved in the slight smile she'd only ever seen him give to her. Before she could speak, he swept her into an embrace.

Turning her head, she placed her hands on his chest. "Stephen, wait."

He brushed his lips over the skin beneath her ear. "Why?"

She couldn't think when he did that. "Because..." Soft kisses along her jaw. "Stephen..." His hands tightened on her back. "Your brother's in there," she blurted.

He froze. Pulling back, he said, "Pardon?"

"Your brother is in the orangery and he's not alone." She cleared her throat. "Lydia Torrence is with him."

Expression blank, he stared at her.

"They are in the orangery. Alone. And they were…embracing." Her cheeks burned. Why was she so embarrassed? So hesitant? Squaring her shoulders, she lifted her chin. "This is an opportunity, Stephen, to obtain the funds you require. We can tell your brother if he doesn't give you the funds, we will make it so all of society will know. Even if society does find out, they will marry anyway. It is a plan without victim, and your charity will benefit."

Still he remained silent, his arms crossed over his chest as his gaze bored into her.

She wet her lips. "Stephen?"

"If I threatened Lydia," he said. "Oliver would never speak to me again."

Oliver. Not Roxwaithe. Not the earl. Oliver.

"He would *never* speak to me again," he continued, still with that strange tone. "He would cut me from his life. It would be as if he never had a brother, or at least, one who was still alive. It would be so that when I see him out in society, at a club, on the street, he would turn the other way and he would pass me by, his gaze never straying in my direction. He would ignore my calls, my letters, and I would be barred entry to Roxegate, to Waithe Hall, to all the Farlisle properties. I would have funds—he would not want me to starve—but I would never again have the skerrick of affection I hold now. He would be done with me. And I would not blame him."

His expression hardened and she recoiled at the look in his eyes. "How could you think I could harm Lydia? She is as a sister to me. She and my thick-headed brother may be stupidly in love with each other and refuse to acknowledge it, but I will not use that for something as petty as a few pounds."

"But you hate your brother." Uncertainty leant a quiver to her voice. "You do hate him, don't you?"

He stared at her stonily. Finally, he shook his head once, sharply.

Horror filled her. She'd made a mistake. She'd—"But…but you said…You tell him lies to collect funds. How can you…?"

"He is my brother. You don't understand. You have never had a family."

Pain tore through her, and she couldn't control the sharp gasp that escaped her.

Uncertainty flickered in his eyes before his expression shuttered. "You will not speak of this. To anyone."

She couldn't speak. She shook her head, her thoughts a jumble.

"Sera, you will not. Swear to me."

"I will not speak of it," she managed.

He studied her a moment, and then nodded sharply before turning to leave.

No. No, he couldn't leave. He couldn't— They had to — She caught his arm. "Stephen—"

He ripped himself from her. "Don't," he said harshly. She recoiled. He closed his eyes briefly. "Don't, Sera," he continued softly and, shaking her off, he strode away.

Cupping her elbows, Sera stared after him. Numb. She needed to be numb. She couldn't—

A noise made her look around. Of course. Perfect. Lydia Torrence. She approached, her chin lifted and her gaze hard.

Sera arranged a mocking smile upon her features though it didn't sit well. "Well, well, if it isn't Lydia Torrence. Whatever are you doing here, Lydia Torrence?"

Lydia squared her shoulders. "Are you crying?"

Sera started, then raised her chin mulishly. "Why are you wandering the halls, or perhaps I can guess? However, I don't really need to. I know it has to do with Lord Roxwaithe."

"You don't know anything."

"I know you were in the orangery. I know you were…close."

Lydia stared at her. "Do you?"

"It would be unfortunate if that knowledge was to become more widely known." What was she doing? Stephen had said he couldn't trust her and, apparently, he was right.

"You know what, Seraphina?" Lydia burst out. "I don't care. Tell my family. Tell everyone. Do you think I care what other people think? Do you think I care what *you* think?"

Sera felt the blood drain from her face. "You don't?"

Lydia held her gaze, refusing to answer.

Sera swallowed. "Why don't you?"

"Because…" Lydia leant close. "I don't like you."

Sera flinched, stricken at her own words thrown back at her. With one final look, Lydia stalked off.

Leaning against the wall, Sera pressed her arms into her stomach. She couldn't think. She couldn't… Why did it matter what Lydia Torrence thought of her? Why did a sharp pain lodge in her chest, and it was all she could do not to scream and scream and scream?

Lightning crashed, and she saw Stephen again before her, looking as if…looking as if…as if he hated her.

She opened her mouth and the strangest sound came out. Was it a moan? A sob? What was happening to her? What was…?

She'd only thought to help. She'd thought to help him, to get him what he wanted. How could he look at her so? *How*?

Tomorrow. She would go to him tomorrow and she would explain. She would tell him she was wrong, she didn't mean it, and…She would explain. He would let her explain. He had to.

He had to.

Chapter Sixteen

STORMING THROUGH ROXEGATE'S HALLS, Stephen reached his brother's study and shoved open the door. "What did you do?"

Oliver's head jerked up, surprise hardening into displeasure. "I'll thank you to lower your voice."

Bloody hell, who cared about his bloody tone? "I shall clarify. What did you do to Lydia Torrence?"

Oliver's hard expression dropped. "What do you mean? Is she hurt?"

Stephen scowled. "Christ, Oliver, what were you thinking?" Probably wasn't thinking, more to the point. Probably couldn't think past the cockstand in his—

"Stephen. Is. She. Hurt?"

His brother's panicked words ripped through his inner rants. Oliver was pale, his fist clenched and knuckles white. Gentling his tone, he said, "No. Not physically, however it was a damn near thing. You're lucky the rumour didn't spread."

Oliver closed his eyes, his throat moving. Stephen watched him compose himself, watched the intense fear slowly recede. His brother really did love Lydia. "What rumour?" Oliver finally asked.

"That you and Lydia—That you—" Uncomfortable, he shifted his weight. Lydia was as a sister to him. He really didn't want to think of her and his brother…and he especially did not want to think on the circumstances surrounding why he knew. Again, he saw Sera's face, stricken and pale. His chest ached.

"What?"

Snapping back to the present, he said, "Don't make me

say it. That you and she were...caught."

"Caught?" Oliver blinked.

How could his brother be so dense? Allegedly, he ran a blasted earldom. "Bloody hell, man, what do you think I mean? Caught."

"We were caught?"

Counting to ten, Stephen braced his hands on the back of the chair. "You mean there was something you could have been caught doing?"

Neck a dull red, Oliver set his jaw. "It is none of your concern."

Irritation bit at him, and he welcomed it. Anything was better than the ache in his chest. "Of course it's my bloody concern. Lydia is like a sister to me. Do you think you're the only one with ties to the Torrences? What were you thinking, Oliver? Couldn't you have just married her first?"

Oliver's gaze jerked to him. "What?"

"We wouldn't be in this mess now. I wouldn't have had to—" The ache deepened as he saw again Sera's desperate, stricken expression. He swallowed.

Oliver shook his head. "I can't marry her."

Stephen passed his hand over his eyes. "Not this again."

"I am too old for her."

"You know she is in love with you."

"She is not. Not really."

Christ above. "Fine. Let us say, for the sake of argument, she is not in love with you. What about you?"

Crossing his arms, Oliver said sullenly, "What about me?"

"You are hers. You've always been hers. You've been on hold, waiting for her. Everyone knows it, but for some reason you refuse to acknowledge it. You won't just bloody admit it." He exhaled. "I am tired of this, brother. I am tired of being your heir. Just marry Lydia, unite our families officially, and set about the business of disinheriting me. You cannot play with her, Oliver."

"I am not playing with her."

"No, I know." His lips twisted bitterly. "This is deadly serious."

"I love her," Oliver said, as if testing out the words.

"Everyone knows that."

A look of wonder lit his face. "I love her."

It was so easy for his brother. The woman he loved also loved him in return. There was nothing keeping them apart but stubbornness. "Marry her."

His brother shook his head. "She deserves more."

"It doesn't matter what you think she deserves. She wants you."

"She only thinks she does. She's too young to know what she wants."

Stephen laughed shortly. "She's known what she's wanted since she was a girl. Why are you so convinced she doesn't know her own mind?"

Bending his head, Oliver stared down at his desk while Stephen stared at him. This was now beyond ridiculous. There was no longer any reason for his brother to keep himself from Lydia. She was grown and she had decided. If he felt the same, he should grasp happiness with both hands.

Sera's face, her eyes wet with tears.

Stephen shoved the image aside. He couldn't trust her. She was willing to deceive and harm his family, and he could not... But what else should she think? He was willing to deceive and harm his family. His brother. Oliver. "I don't want to study the occult," he said abruptly.

Oliver blinked. "Pardon?"

"I don't want to study the occult." Swallowing, he said softly, "I wanted money."

"I beg your pardon?"

He shifted uncomfortably. "I knew you wouldn't give me funds outright, not if I told you what they were really for, so...I lied."

"You lied."

"Yes."

"Why?"

Stomach churning, he met his brother's gaze. "It's worked before."

Oliver stared at him. The clock ticked on the mantle, loud in the silence of the study.

His brother took a slow, steadying breath. "I see. So what was your plan to secure funds..." Stephen saw the moment comprehension dawned. "You would feign interest in a plan even an idiot would know was doomed to failure. Once I'd refused to release your funds, you would wait a few weeks and then apply again, this time with a much more reasonable request."

"And you would agree."

Oliver nodded. "What did you want it for this time?"

His brother was calm. Too calm. His gaze was steady, his face composed. It would be so much better if he yelled. "I wanted to start a football team."

"A football team."

"For workhouse children. It was to have been a charitable foundation to improve their circumstances. We thought to encourage them to attend the parish school with a certain degree of attendance, have it as a requirement to play in the competition— I wanted to help. I do not have many skills, but I know football and—" Bloody hell, he was rambling. "I wanted money for a football team."

"So, you lied so you could start a charity."

"Yes, Oliver. I lied to start a charity."

Eyes hard, Oliver rubbed his chin. "Did you not think to talk to me about this? Did you not think I would not want to help? Christ, Stephen, if not because you're my brother, but because it would be the decent thing to do?"

"You have never helped before," he said resentfully.

Disbelief writ Oliver's face. "It is all I do."

"Not without a goddamn argument!" he shouted. Composing himself, he continued intensely, "You never support me. You don't believe I have any idea how to handle finances or what might be best for me. Christ. Is it any wonder you won't believe Lydia either?"

"Do not bring her into this," Oliver said dangerously.

"Why not? You behave in the exact same way with both of us."

"Lydia didn't attempt to extort money from me."

"No. She just wanted your heart, but you won't allow her, will you? You'd rather play us all, puppets tangled in your strings, begging for scraps."

"Don't presume you know my mind, brother," Oliver said, sounding exactly like their father.

Stephen snapped straight. "Yes. Of course. My lord," he said coldly.

Oliver opened his mouth to respond, but before he could, the door to the study opened. Irritated, Stephen jerked his head around.

Standing there, with his hand in Alexandra Torrence's,

was Maxim.

He blinked. No. It couldn't be. His younger brother was dead. Maxim had been fifteen and died at sea. Maxim was dead.

A roaring started in Stephen's ears. He stared dumbly as his dead brother walked into the room, as he and Oliver spoke, as he clung to Alexandra Torrence's hand. This man grown couldn't be his brother. He couldn't be. He couldn't...

But it was. It was Maxim. Maxim grown into a man.

And he was speaking of their father.

"What did Father say?"

All three of them—Oliver, Alexandra and, god, Maxim—looked at him. Setting his jaw, Stephen repeated, "What did Father say?"

Maxim glanced at Alexandra, who smiled reassuringly. "He said not to return. He said my shame was too great."

"What shame?" Stephen asked.

Maxim shook his head.

"What shame?" he pressed.

Oliver said, "Perhaps we should—"

"No," Stephen said sharply. "What shame?"

"Stephen," Oliver said. "Our brother has just returned. How does this matter?"

"It matters!" Emotion—confusion, relief, shock, Bloody hell, Maxim wasn't dead—erupted. "It bloody matters. Maxim died, Oliver. He died and now he's back and—" He choked. Shoulders shaking, he turned away.

"Father said he would disown me," Maxim answered. "Because I was sent down from Eton for cheating, but I didn't cheat. I paid someone to write my assignments, but I dictated every word, and the reason I did that... The reason... I can't...I can't read.

"You can read," Alexandra said fiercely.

"But not well," he said softly. "Not well."

He couldn't sort it out in his head. Maxim couldn't read? He had cheated at Eton?

"Perhaps not, but we are seeking help," Alexandra said. "George will know of a treatment, and if he doesn't, he will know someone who can." She scowled. "Maxim is not stupid."

"Of course not," Oliver said.

Alexandra firmed her chin, her expression still fierce.

"This is why you and Father fought?" Oliver said.

Maxim nodded. "He said I should not return home. He

said I should become a ship-hand on a Roxwaithe ship, and so I did. I... It was a bull-headed move."

"Father was the bull-headed one," Stephen said sullenly.

"He was wrong," Oliver ran a hand over his hair. "Father was wrong. You should never have been made to feel you should have left, and that you were ever not welcome when you returned. You need never be unsure of your welcome, Maxim. You are always welcome." He shook his head. "Maxim. You are alive."

The corner of his younger brother's lip twitched. "I am."

Oliver started to laugh. A smile stole across Maxim's face and Alexandra beamed, looking between the three of them.

Stephen's own smile felt forced. "I...have an appointment. I—" Unable to finish the sentence, he left.

He didn't remember the passage from Oliver's study but somehow he ended up in the bedchamber that had once been his. Running a hand over his mouth, he stared at the furnishings that had replaced his bed, his dresser, his wardrobe. He looked at the curtains that were not his, the muted green walls when he preferred blue, and the years that separated the time he'd last set foot in this room and now.

The years when Maxim had been alive.

Back against the wall, he sank to the floor. Maxim was alive. His brother was alive.

Cheeks wet, he laughed harshly. One of the great tragedies of his life turned out to be a complete falsehood. Thumping the back of his head against the wall, he closed his eyes. Maxim was alive.

The corner of his mouth tipped up, and then he laughed. He laughed and he laughed until he was sick with the sound, and he didn't know what to do, what came next, how it was possible Maxim was alive.

Hanging his head, he curled his arms around his knees. Maxim was alive...but Harbor was still dead. Would that Harbor had also walked through the door. Would that both his brother and his friend were never dead. Would that, when Stephen realised his brother was not dead, all he had felt was joy...and not resentment that Harbor wasn't by his side.

Chapter Seventeen

Sera pulled her cloak tighter to her body. The late November sun shone brightly but the wind was bitterly cold, cutting through to her skin and stinging her cheeks.

Beside her, Miss Edirisinghe chattered brightly, her arm looped through Sera's as they walked down the high street. "I had no notion of the cold! It really is quite chilling, straight to the bone. I am glad for you allowing me to borrow this cloak. I shall have to purchase cloth for one when we reach the linen-drapers! It is so strange to think of such things. It does not get this cold back home, and I'm quite certain I shall only use this when I am in London, but I will come often now we know of each other. Oh, I am so looking forward to it already!"

Miss Edirisinghe continued her chatter, holding the conversation by herself. Sera was glad of such. She did not feel much like socialising these three months gone.

Gatherings had dried up with the approach of winter. Most of society had retreated to their country homes, and to tell it true, Sera had been glad. She did not feel much like attending balls and pretending she was enjoying herself. A pile of correspondence sat on her desk, invitations to what gatherings there were amongst them. She would respond to them soon. Maybe.

She had not seen much of Maria and Elizabeth either. Maria spent her time with her new fiancé and his family, while Elizabeth had left for the Continent over a month ago. Sera found herself at loose ends and, with a need to distract herself, she'd sought to do so with the girl who was her sister.

At first, she'd thought she would take the girl as a

project, introduce her to society, and guide her through its pitfalls. Instead, Miss Edirisinghe had come to Tidswell House and they had spent day after day in the parlour, getting to know one another as Miss Edirisinghe chattered brightly and produced piece after terrible piece of embroidery. Sera now knew more about her father than she'd ever had, certainly more than the stilted quarterly letters she had received from him. She also knew of her half-brothers, her stepmother, and all the occupants of Miss Edirisinghe's life in Ceylon. Miss Edirisinghe shared of herself freely and without guile, and Sera had found herself holding her tongue when a sharp comment had occurred, instead listening as Miss Edirisinghe invited her to journey through her life.

Strangely, Sera found her chatter calming, and it had become that she looked forward to the visits, even with Miss Edirisinghe's silent chaperone lurking in the background.

Today was one of the few occasions they had ventured outside Tidswell House, and only because Miss Edirisinghe had so admired Sera's latest ball gown. She'd been present for the delivery, and the delight on the girl's face and prompted Sera to offer to show her where she had acquired the fabric. Thus, they now found themselves on the high street making their way to the linen-draper.

It had also been three months since she had spoken with Stephen.

Shaking herself, she focussed instead on Miss Edirisinghe's chatter.

"What are you hoping to purchase, Lady Seraphina? Fabric for another gown as beautiful as your last? Perhaps something in blue? You do look so well in blue, especially royal blue. Do you think you will pick this colour? Oh, do you think you will let me pick the colour? I would do so well to pick your gown, and it would be such an honour…"

A gust of wind raised goose bumps on her arm. Overhead, grey clouds threatened. It was fortunate it would not be long before they reached the linen-draper.

"Did you hear the Earl and the soon-to-be Countess of Roxwaithe's are to hold a house party at the earl's seat in Yorkshire to celebrate their marriage?"

Sera's head whipped around.

"Everyone is simply dying for an invitation to Waithe Hall and thus their marriage," her sister continued, oblivious to her reaction. "It's an ever-so-romantic story, don't you think? Growing up in neighbouring estates, falling in love. It is the same with his brother and her sister, isn't it? Although, there is an added romance to theirs—Lord Maxim Farlisle returned from the dead and then they fell in love! Do you think they will be there? I am unsure—"

"Have you received an invitation?" she asked suddenly, and thought of the pile of correspondence on her desk.

Miss Edirisinghe stopped mid-sentence, eyes wide with surprise. "Oh, no, of course not. They have kept the guest list small, and I do not believe I have made the acquaintance of neither the earl nor Lady Lydia Torrence. Do you think it is a small party because of Lord Maxim? Do you think he will be there? But he must be, he is the earl's brother. It is all anyone can talk about, his return. Do you remember his disappearance? I was speaking with Miss Bartlett and she said it was all anyone could talk about, a tragedy turned into a miracle. You were being courted by Lord Stephen Farlisle, were you not? Did he say anything about it? I cannot believe we have not spoken of this before!"

"No, we haven't," she agreed softly.

Miss Edirisinghe clearly saw nothing wrong in that answer and sought nothing further, continuing with her chatter. Unfortunately, the girl's brightness no longer had the power to distract Sera from her thoughts. From thinking on Stephen.

She had seen him a few times in the time since that disastrous last meet, more flashes in the distance than anything of substance.

All of London had been afire with the return from the dead of Lord Maxim Farlisle. Everyone had invited the Farlisles to their soirees, though they were almost uniformly refused. The family had kept to themselves, such that the marriage of Lord Maxim to Lady Alexandra Torrence had not been announced until two weeks after the fact and the couple had departed for the family estate in Yorkshire. Any notes requesting an audience had been politely refused, and even when she'd called upon Stephen's bachelor residence, fighting her way through the opportunists and the gawkers and those who recalled she and Stephen's connection and tried to pry information from her, she'd been turned away. The butler, though, had churlishly informed her Lord Stephen Farlisle was not in attendance and it might be best for her to contact Roxegate House. Defeated, she had returned home, and the days had become weeks, and the weeks months, and now it was too much time had passed between that last moment and this, and she could not see a way to fix what had broken between them.

Society, deprived of new opportunities to whisper and gossip about the Farlisles, had turned attention elsewhere: Always, new scandals rose to take the place of the last: the beauteous Lady Sarah Hartlett had been found in a compromising position with an unassuming nobody, while Mrs Dalloway had attempted to shoot Lord Carow in a lovers' quarrel. With the advent of such, London had quite forgotten the return of a dead man, but they would be reminded once the invitations to Waithe Hall and the wedding of Lady Lydia Torrence to the Earl of Roxwaithe started to appear.

Her mind ticked over. There would be a way to attend…Surely Lydia would not refuse a request from Miss Edirisinghe? Her sister was sweet and well-liked, and why wouldn't she be wanted? If Miss Edirisinghe managed an invitation, she would want to bring her elder sister, who had navigated society for years and was only looking out for her newly found younger sibling.

And then, finally, she could speak with Stephen

"Would you like to attend?" she asked suddenly.

Miss Edirisinghe's chatter stopped abruptly. "Attend?"

"The house party at Waithe Hall. I am certain they would be delighted to have your presence."

Confusion creasing her brow, Miss Edirisinghe said haltingly, "But I have not received an invitation."

Sera waved her hand. "That is of no concern. One does not require an invitation."

"I do not understand, Lady Seraphina. What do you mean?"

"If you wish to attend, I can arrange it so you can. Imagine being able to tell everyone you were present at such an exclusive event. They would be so envious, and you would be certain to be invited to every social occasion in town."

Her brow creased further. "I cannot think it proper. Also, Father has stipulated I am to remain in London for the duration of my time in England."

"But surely you wish to attend?" she cajoled. "An earl's wedding celebration? It is sure to be astounding."

"More than like, but I really should adhere to the rules.

Father would force me home if I do not."

"Father doesn't have to know."

Miss Edirisinghe regarded her uncertainly. "Well...I suppose not."

"Come. It would be fun."

"Yes, I suppose it would, but I'm not sure..."

Sera suddenly realised what she was doing. How could she seek to deceive this young lady...seek to deceive her sister? Miss Edirisinghe had been nothing but kind, and Sera sought to manipulate and harm. Just as Stephen said.

Eyes stinging, she smiled brightly. "No, you are quite right. You should not go against Father's wishes."

Miss Edirisinghe looked thoroughly confused. "But why then did you say—"

"It is of no matter. Please, I beg you forget I ever spoke of such."

"Of course." Miss Edirisinghe was silent a moment. "Is it because of Lord Stephen?"

Shock held Sera's tongue. "What do you mean?" she finally managed.

"You were courting, were you not? And then something must have happened, as you are no longer."

"I—" She could think of no way to respond.

"It would have been something more than Lord Stephen's brother returning from the dead. If it was solely that, he would have turned to you for comfort. It was something else, something like—" She cocked her head. "Did it have something to do with Lady Lydia Torrence?"

She cleared her throat. "Why do you say that?"

"You were not always nice to her."

Sera couldn't believe she was so transparent. Miss Edirisinghe watched her with a gentle smile, as if she hadn't just seen straight through Sera's machinations to the truth of the matter. "What do you mean?"

"Sera." Miss Edirisinghe's smile turned kind. "You are not always at your best."

She stared at her. This girl, who she'd thought was simple and innocent, saw so much. "No, I'm not." She licked her lips. "I'm trying, though."

"I know." Miss Edirisinghe smiled encouragingly. "You'll do better."

Unable to speak, Sera stared at her. How was it this girl

had such faith in her? No one in her life had ever given her encouragement, or urged her to be better. No one had…cared.

Stephen's half-smile flashed before her. She rubbed at her chest.

"You know, if you wish to attend the wedding celebrations, you should just ask. I'm sure they would extend an invitation," Miss Edirisinghe continued, looping her arm through Sera's as she resumed her pace.

"But it is as you said. I was not kind to Lady Lydia."

"No. But forgiveness has to start somewhere." Miss Edirisinghe looked at the sky. "It is starting to rain."

Sera held out her hand. A drop fell on the leather of her glove, beading and clinging to the surface. "The linen-drapers is not far."

Miss Edirisinghe grinned. "Shall we rush?"

At Sera's nod, Miss Edirisinghe tugged her into a run, giggling all the while.

They entered the linen-draper's, shaking the rain from them. Miss Edirisinghe grinned at her. "I am to the wools."

Shaking her cloak, Sera watched as the girl dashed off. An assistant approached and offered a drying cloth, which Sera accepted gladly, and she idly examined cloth swatches until she heard Miss Edirisinghe's voice. "I do not understand. Why can you not assist me?"

The shop assistant froze. "I…have to get Mrs Penn."

Sera frowned.

A moment later, a woman who presumably was Mrs Penn appeared. "We are appreciative of you attending our establishment, but perhaps a different shop would be better suited to…you."

Miss Edirisinghe's smile dimmed, her shoulders falling slightly. "I see."

Well, Sera didn't see. This woman would serve her sister and be grateful of it.

It took less than a moment to be at her sister's side. "I do not believe you know to whom you speak," Sera said as haughtily as she could manage.

"Sera, don't." Gaze averted, her sister's ever-present smile had disappeared.

"She will not be allowed to continue this disrespect." She turned to the woman. "You address Lady Charuni Edirisinghe-Waller, daughter to the Marquess of Tidswell. I am her sister,

Lady Seraphina Waller-Mitchell."

The woman's gaze darted between them. "I cannot in good conscience allow her kind in my shop. You understand, my lady."

"No. I do not understand. Explain it to me."

"Well, because she— That is to say— She would be better with her own kind."

"Her own kind, madam? She is with her own kind."

Her sister laid a hand on her forearm. "Sera."

Sera fell silent.

Her sister looked at the woman. "You make a mistake…Mrs Penn, was it? It is as my sister says, I am the daughter of an English marquess." She smiled gently. "I am ever so sorry, but I did not realise your shop was not for the those of the peerage. My sister and I will let it be known amongst our circle, and I'm sure word will quickly spread. It will be that none of the peerage frequent your establishment—none of my kind, as you said. I thank you for the education."

"No, but…I didn't mean…" the woman spluttered.

"Oh? Then what did you mean?"

Impotently, the woman stared at them.

Charuni smiled again. "I bid you good day." She turned to Sera. "Shall we depart?"

They had left the linen-draper and were walking down the street—thankfully, it had stopped raining— before Sera spoke. "I cannot believe her. What a terrible woman."

"She is not unusual."

Sera stopped and stared at her sister. "What do you mean?"

Charuni smiled. "I am a brown-skinned girl in a country of pale English roses. I knew what to expect. Father's privilege affords me some protection, but it is not absolute."

"I had no idea."

"Why would you?" Charuni was silent a moment. "You called me your sister."

"Well, we share a father. I would say that makes us related."

"You have never before called me sister."

"Well, I—" Sera's mind went blank. That was…true. Sera regarded her sister uncertainly. What had changed?

"Why did you say my name had Waller in it?" Charuni asked, saving her from thinking on it further.

"Doesn't it?"

Her sister shook her head. "We have always gone by my mother's name. Why would it not be Waller-Mitchell?"

She could answer this easily. "That is not Father's name. Part of the marriage settlement was for any issue of their union to be named both Father's and Grandfather's names, with Grandfather's as the final name. He was a wily one, wanting an heir to the marquessate to have a merchant's name."

"But my brother is heir the marquessate."

"Yes. More fool dear old Grandfather."

"So your grandfather insisted on something that would strike a blow at Father's pride."

"Yes. That is one way to look at it."

"And your mother left you when you were a baby."

"Yes."

"And then Father…"

Ignoring the ache in her chest, she said impatiently, "What are you intimating, Charuni?"

Stopping dead on the street, Charuni hugged her. "I am sorry your family is horrible."

Caught off guard, Sera looked around them. What few people remained on the street after the rain had not noticed the two of them or, if they had, they'd paid them no mind. Hesitantly, she returned her sister's embrace. Is this what Stephen meant? When he said she had no notion of what family was? Was family simply someone who hugged you when you were sad? Was family those people you would kill for? In this moment, she would destroy anyone who thought to harm her sister. She would use every weapon at her considerable disposal to make it so her sister was never harmed and, with every fibre of her being, she would protect her.

Comprehension dawned. This. This is why Stephen would never betray his brother.

Pulling back, Charuni said, "You know, you could just invite yourself to the wedding celebration."

Ducking her head, she hid the tears clouding her eyes. "I beg your pardon?"

"As you said before—is there not a way?"

Sera stared at her sister. Charuni stared back guilelessly, as if she had not suggested a devious plan, as if she had not just turned the tables on a bigoted shop-owner.

A smile tugged at Sera. Perhaps she and her sister were

more alike than she'd thought.

But when she got home and looked at the pile of correspondence on her desk, she found she did not need to employ the plan Charuni suggested. For sitting there, in a pristine cream envelope, was an invitation to the wedding of Lady Lydia Torrence and the Earl of Roxwaithe.

Chapter Eighteen

CONCENTRATING FIERCELY, STEPHEN TAPPED the football with his left knee to bounce off his chest, catching it with his right foot. He flicked his ankle and the round ball rose again, hitting his right knee only for him to tap it again to bounce off his chest, this time catching it with his left foot.

Again and again, he repeated the actions. It had snowed again overnight, coating Waithe Hall and its surrounds in white. With the snow three inches deep and as Stephen had no desire to break an ankle, he'd reverted to the indoor pitch of his youth and made his way to the Long Gallery. No one in residence at Waithe Hall would bother him up here, and he'd needed the soothing only football could bring. He had, after all, endured yet another week of Oliver's company.

Three weeks they'd been at the Farlisle ancestral estate in Yorkshire, reacquainting themselves with Waithe Hall and its surrounds. After Maxim's disappearance and their father's death, Oliver had shuttered the hall and removed to London, making it so years had passed without a visit. On the rare occasion Stephen had needed to come to Yorkshire, he'd stayed at Bentley Close, the Marquis of Demartine's residence bordering theirs. Alexandra and Maxim had arrived ahead of them all, ensuring Waithe Hall was prepared for the family and guests. They had married quietly six weeks ago, and they saw no need to celebrate their marriage in the way Lydia and Oliver intended to.

Stephen hadn't seen his younger brother in over two months, not that he'd seen him much prior to that. Maxim and Oliver had been holed up in the study, going through the requirements of Maxim's return from the dead and avoiding those who sought to fodder for their gossip. Roxegate had no shortage of visitors once word of Maxim's return got out, though all were turned away. Stephen wasn't sure if that had been a solid move or not. The lack of response leant weight to the mystery, and there were no doubt dozens of rumours circulating based on nothing but supposition.

Less than a week after Maxim's return, it had become clear Stephen could no longer reside at his lodgings. He'd resisted returning to Roxegate as long as he could, but when the other residents of his lodgings had issued a thinly disguised threat for him to depart the premises due to the constant bombardment of gawkers, he'd reluctantly packed a trunk and moved to his family's townhouse. Once in residence, he'd avoided Oliver as much as possible: taking his breakfast in his room; avoiding the study and its surrounds; making his way to the pitch to train with Franco and the lads as much as he could. He'd not yet returned to the 1810 Club. He had no desire to hear Sutton's comments, or face pity from the others. Ash had tried to visit a few times, but Stephen had refused his card. He didn't want to think on them. He didn't want to think on them, then think on Maxim's return, and then realise over again how Harbor never would.

As for his little brother, he'd barely seen him since his return, and never alone. Maxim was like a ghost still, talked of in whispers and his lack of presence leaving a vacuum. Stephen saw him at dinner, when they awkwardly sat at the table to eat as quickly as possible and then to retire to separate rooms. On the nights attended by the Torrences—each daughter affianced to his elder and younger brothers—conversation flowed, though he felt awkward and out of place. But then, he'd always felt awkward and out of place.

And now they were here at Waithe Hall to celebrate Oliver and Lydia's marriage.

Grey cat's eyes, dark hair and a wicked smile flashed before him before he forced her away.

Letting the ball fall to the floor, Stephen kicked it viciously and, exhaling harshly, he went to collect it. It had rolled to a stop under one of the windows that lined the hall, any number of which he and his brothers had smashed over the years with footballs, cricket balls, croquet balls and, on one memorable occasion, a horseshoe. Perhaps it was not the wisest choice of venue, with windows lining one wall and the portraits of their forebears the other, but the length had proven irresistible to them as boys.

His gaze snagged on a dent in the panelling beside the window. Oliver had smashed a cricket ball off of Maxim's bowl straight into the panelling, leaving a dent that remained to this day. One of the tables still wobbled from when they'd used it as a football goal, Stephen having clipped a leg with a stupendous bending strike that Oliver had had no chance of defending. There might even still be drops of blood in the carpet from Maxim's split lip that had swelled to twice its size, causing Lady Demartine to cluck and fuss when she'd discovered the injury. Lady Demartine had taken care of all their bumps and bruises, their father abdicating the responsibility to reside most of each year in London. It was safe to say Stephen knew Alexandra and Lydia's mother better than his own parent. A hundred memories existed in this place, back before Maxim had disappeared, and the three of them were truly brothers.

"Stephen."

He stiffened. At the other end of the hall, his younger brother stood with his arms crossed over his broad chest, his expression guarded. Would Harbor have looked like that, displayed that wariness, if he now stood in Maxim's place? Something twinged in his chest, but ruthlessly he suppressed it. "Maxim."

His brother was much changed since his return. It was probably always going to happen, even if Maxim hadn't gone through what he had in the last eleven years: A shipwreck, memory loss, illness, destitution, harsh labour, and then finally a return to England. He was silent a great deal, and he spent most of his company in Alexandra's, apart from when Oliver required him.

"I thought I would be the only one here," Maxim said.

"Well," he said. "You aren't."

"I can see that." Maxim's hands tightened on his abnormally large biceps. When had Maxim grown a broad chest? In Stephen's memory, his brother was reed-thin, and he couldn't reconcile this burly, towering man with the slight boy he remembered. "What are you doing?"

"Water colours."

Maxim glanced at the football. "Clearly." Moving closer, he continued, "Are you hiding, too?"

"No," Stephen replied automatically.

"So the fact dozens of people are now occupying Waithe Hall doesn't set your teeth on edge?"

Stephen worked his jaw. Maxim stared at him, as if he could see exactly how much the steady stream of people into Waithe Hall unnerved him. "Maybe," he finally conceded.

"It sets *my* teeth on edge. Alexandra is busy all the time with wedding preparation. I find myself at loose ends, and there are all these *people* staring at me and whispering and—" He shuddered.

"It's to be expected," Stephen said. "You *have* returned from the dead."

Maxim grimaced. "This is almost more trouble than it's worth. If it weren't for Alexandra, I might have just cut my losses and run."

"Oliver and I don't factor into your decision?"

Maxim's dark eyes—so like Stephen's own—jerked up to meet his. "I didn't mean it like that. I—" He raked a hand through his hair. "I apologise."

Stephen shrugged. "No need. We're practically strangers."

Maxim laughed shortly. "Bloody hell, I remember that. You and your bloody contrariness."

"Well, pardon the hell out of me. I'm sorry we don't know each other. I'm sorry we're practically strangers. It wouldn't matter anyway. It seems the Farlisle men are doomed to estrangement."

Brows drawing, Maxim cocked his head. "What do you mean?"

"Nothing," he muttered.

"Is it Father? Is it how he always…He would stay in London, wouldn't he? And we would remain here. We never joined him…or did we? Sometimes, I misremember things." He exhaled shakily. "Sometimes I don't remember at all."

Stephen frowned. "I thought you had recovered your memories."

"Not all of them. Apparently, it doesn't work like that. You know, I didn't remember Alexandra at all at first."

Surprise filled him. Maxim and Alexandra had been joined at the hip when they were children, and to see them now made it hard to believe Maxim had ever forgotten her. "Truly? You didn't remember her?"

A slight smile tugging at his mouth, Maxim nodded. "She wasn't too impressed with that, but then I remembered and she, uh—" Cheeks ruddy, he cleared his throat. "Alexandra says I might remember it all, or I might not. She has been in correspondence with doctors specialising in my condition. She's quite determined," he said with a faint smile.

The amusement and warmth in his brother's voice…how was it mere months after his return he'd fallen in love and married? He told himself the emotion he felt wasn't jealousy. "Do you remember how to play football?" he finally asked.

Maxim grinned. "Maybe."

"Think fast, then." And he struck the ball at his brother, rushing after it to attempt to steal it back. Maxim blocked him with his body, manoeuvring the ball between his feet to keep it from Stephen.

They jostled, each trying to take control of the ball. Stephen shouldered Maxim's chest but his brother was unyielding, absorbing the attack and keeping the ball from Stephen's control. A grin flashed over Maxim's face and Stephen felt an answering one tug at him, exhilaration flooding him as he attempted another steal.

"Are you trying to destroy my hall?"

They both skidded to a halt. Oliver stood at the opposite end of the Long Gallery, and all the enjoyment Stephen felt fled.

"No more than when we were boys," Maxim said. Stephen said nothing, stilling the ball with his foot.

"So what are you doing?"

"Playing football. Why are *you* here?" Maxim asked.

For a long moment, Oliver stared at them and then, averting his gaze, mumbled something.

"What was that?"

"There are too many people," he said.

Stephen and Maxim exchanged a glance. Maxim laughed, and Stephen gave an unwilling smile.

"What?" Oliver demanded.

Maxim shook his head. "It seems to be hereditary."

Oliver looked between them. "You, too?"

Still grinning, Maxim nodded. Stephen shrugged.

Oliver shoved a hand through his hair. Strands had fallen from his queue, brushing his shoulders and speaking eloquently of his discomfort. "Christ, I didn't know it would be like this when Lydia said she wanted a wedding here at Waithe Hall. I thought it would be our family and the Torrences, and then maybe a dozen guests. Did you know all the available beds in the village are full, as is Bentley Close? We have twenty-four people staying here, in addition to us. Bloody hell, people are even travelling in from *York*. It's too much. Too much." He shook his head. "I haven't even *seen* Lydia in three days. I just want the wedding part over and done with. You had the right idea, Maxim. Should have just bloody eloped."

"But the earl must have an elaborate ceremony," Stephen said. Because of course he must.

Oliver exhaled. "I don't even care about that. I just want Lydia to be my wife. I want to go to sleep with her at night and wake in the morning with her in my arms. I want *our* life to start. Christ. This is a nightmare."

"Being married *is* pretty excellent," Maxim said.

Oliver threw him a tart look. "That's right, brother. Brag away."

Maxim smirked.

"Right. Well. Might as well do something while we're here." Picking up a side table, Oliver placed it in the middle of the hall. "First one to goal gets a guinea."

Stephen laced his hands and stretched. His brothers might as well give him the guinea now.

It took a moment but for them to slip into old patterns. Oliver guarded the goal, Maxim took position between, and Stephen stood with his foot on the ball, waiting for the signal to begin. Oliver shouted, "Whistle!" and the game began.

Maxim attacked, trying to force Stephen backward and in to making a mistake. He dodged his brother, shifting the ball from one foot to the other with lightning speed, such that Maxim had no idea where Stephen intended to connect with the ball to drive it down the gallery. Maxim attempted a bump, but Stephen spun into it, using the momentum to outpace his brother.

Now, there was only Oliver between him and the goal. Oliver was too far out, leaving the goal unguarded on the left. Stephen feinted right, and then bent the ball around Oliver, striking the ball precisely where he wanted it—straight through the legs of the table to score.

Jogging to a halt, he said, "I'll take that guinea now."

Oliver and Maxim looked at each other and then back at him. "I didn't know you were so good at football," Oliver said.

Stephen shrugged.

Oliver scowled. "Stephen, I'm trying to pay you a compliment."

"Yes, a backhanded one. *I didn't know you were good at football*," he mimicked. "You don't know much, do you? I play football most Saturdays, and train at least twice a week. Of course I'm bloody good at it."

"You do?" Maxim asked in surprise.

"What do I know?" Oliver snapped. "I'll tell you what I know. I know you regularly attempt fraud against the Roxwaithe estate. These last few months I may have been distracted, but we *will* discuss it."

"I don't *attempt* anything."

"You told me—to my *face*—you lie to receive funds."

Stephen smiled thinly. "Like I said. I don't attempt anything. You gave me the funds, each and every time."

Oliver gave him a look of disbelief and then, suddenly, threw the football at him. It hit Stephen in the chest and, stunned, he caught it. "What was that for?"

"What is your problem?" his brother shouted.

"I don't have a problem," he shouted back.

"You do. You blasted well do. Just tell me!"

"Why? So you can lecture me?"

"Bloody hell, Stephen!"

Holding the football between his hands, he shrugged.

"And that's another thing." Oliver gestured at the ball. "Why didn't you ever tell me you played football?"

Stephen shrugged. "Would you have cared?"

"Of course I bloody care! I would have come to your bloody games!" Oliver exploded.

Stephen shrugged again.

"Fuck, Stephen, you are impossible!"

Stephen blinked. He'd never heard Oliver use such strong language. "You wouldn't have cared, Oliver, and don't pretend you would have come to my matches. You decided a long time ago who I was, and there was no swaying you."

"You never bloody tried!"

"What would have been the point?"

"The point? You're my bloody brother and I bloody love you."

He snorted. "Sure you do."

"What do you mean?" Oliver said dangerously.

Stephen shrugged.

"Stop fucking shrugging!"

Stephen caught his eye and then, deliberately, shrugged.

With a great roar, Oliver launched at him.

Surprise held Stephen still and, when Oliver threw a wild punch, it glanced of his jaw. Anger flared, harsh and bright, and he balled his hand into a fist, catching Oliver in the stomach. Oliver grunted and then charged him, locking them in a grapple. He managed to clip Oliver in the jaw in return, while his brother dug his hand into his shoulder.

Suddenly, they were pulled apart and, dazed, Stephen found himself in a headlock. "That's enough," Maxim said.

Christ, he'd forgotten his younger brother was there, he was so focused on his elder. Glancing over, he saw Maxim had Oliver in a head lock with his other arm. He struggled, but he couldn't get free. Jesus, was his younger brother really that strong?

"I'm not letting go until you both sort this out," Maxim continued.

Stephen swore. Christ, what was his brother about?

Oliver seemed to agree. "What do you know, Maxim?"

"I know apparently you two haven't had a frank conversation since I've been gone," he said. "If I have to muscle you into it, then I bloody well will."

This was humiliating. His younger brother held him in a stranglehold and no matter how he twisted, he couldn't get free.

Of a sudden, Oliver wrenched against Maxim's grasp. Maxim absorbed it easily. Well, at least Stephen wasn't the only one who couldn't break their younger brother's hold.

"Are you going to talk to each other?" Maxim asked.

A beat of silence and then— "Fine," Oliver said.

Maxim turned to Stephen.

It burned. It really did.

"Stephen?"

"Fine," he said sullenly.

Maxim let them go and Stephen immediately backed away, rubbing his neck. Oliver rotated his shoulder, looking at anything except his brothers.

"Now," Maxim crossed his arms over his broad chest. "Talk."

Still rubbing his neck, Stephen stared at Oliver. His brother didn't look at him, his gaze averted.

"You're a blockhead, you know," Stephen said.

Oliver's gaze jerked up. "What?"

"A complete arse. Always have been."

Fury stormed across Oliver's face. "What are you, twelve?"

Stephen shrugged.

Oliver's face darkened. "Don't. Shrug."

"Why *do* you shrug?" Maxim asked curiously.

"There's no point doing anything else. He won't listen."

Oliver immediately interrupted with, "I always listen—"

Maxim held up his hand. With a scowl, Oliver fell silent.

"You want to know why I 'defrauded' you, Oliver?" Emotion erupted, years and years of resentment. "I want to help people. I want to make up for my misspent youth and *help*. You wouldn't believe me, so I had to lie. Those funds go to charities," he continued intensely. "There are five charities I help run, and *that's* where my inheritance has gone. I bought that manor for Doctor Griffiths's institute, which helps rehabilitate soldiers with war injuries amongst others. Another allows children—especially girls—get an education they might not otherwise have received. I'm working on a charity where children play in a football league they can only enter if they attend a certain amount of school lessons every quarter. *That* is where the funds I've 'defrauded' from you have gone."

Oliver stared at him. "You've never—"

"I did. I did attempt to discuss it. You cut me off. You never *listen* to me."

"You go out of your way to vex me. I was just trying to steer you on the right course."

"I don't need your bloody steering."

"I didn't *know* that. You never told me you did any of those things. You allowed me to think you a spendthrift, that you were spending money like water. I thought—Christ, Stephen I thought you needed *some* guidance."

"Why?"

Oliver swallowed. "Stephen, you almost died."

Stephen blinked. "What?"

"I couldn't lose you, Stephen. I couldn't have another brother die."

Silence. Stephen stared at his brother. "How did you know that?"

"I came to see you. When you were convalescing."

"But…You…" When? When had his brother come? He

had no memory of it, had thought Oliver had no idea…

"I saw you, lying in that bed, your face bruised and your body broken and I—" His voice cracked.

"Why did you never say anything?"

He ran his hand over his hair, tugged at the knot gathered at his nape. "What would have been the point?"

Bloody hell. They really were both as bad as each other.

"You almost died?"

He looked up. Maxim stared at him, shock drawing his features. Stephen smiled wanly. "But I didn't."

"Jesus." Maxim wiped a hand over his jaw. "We're quite the family."

"Dear lord, are you all attempting to kill each other?"

They all looked over. Lydia Torrence glared back at them.

Stephen shook his head. He'd come to the Long Gallery because he thought he would be alone. Instead, first Maxim had arrived, then Oliver, and now Lydia. He should have camped out in the Entrance Hall, there would have been less traffic.

Oliver straightened. "Stephen started it."

Lydia shot him a look. Oliver gave her a sheepish grin as he worked his jaw, wincing slightly as he did so.

Rubbing his neck, Stephen flexed the bruised knuckles on his other hand. Only Maxim looked relaxed, as if he hadn't just held both Stephen and Oliver in a headlock.

"In any event, dinner will be served in an hour. We have guests, so I trust you will all be presentable for company by then?" Her voice wavered slightly, and her smile was too bright.

Immediately, Oliver went to her. "Lydia, what's wrong?"

Her bright smile brightened. "Nothing."

Oliver frowned. "There is something wrong."

"Why did I think I could keep anything from you?" Lydia's smile wobbled. "Seraphina Waller-Mitchell has arrived."

Stephen froze.

Scowling, Oliver said. "Why is Seraphina Waller-Mitchell here?"

"I may have sent her an invitation," Lydia said in a small voice.

Oliver stared at her in disbelief. "For the love of god, why?"

"Because she's horrible and she taunted me that we

would never be wed and now we are about to be wed and I wanted to rub it in her face," she burst out.

Oliver blinked. "Oh. Well. Valid reason."

"No, it's not." Burying her head in his chest, she mumbled something. Oliver's arms came up to surround her in an embrace as he murmured something back.

Stephen stared at them. Christ. Sera. Here.

He didn't know what to think. An ache opened in his chest, one he'd thought had disappeared but he now realised never had. He'd ignored it, told himself he didn't miss her, didn't ache for her, but he did. God almighty, he did.

And now she was here.

Abruptly, he turned his heel and strode from the Long Gallery, ignoring Maxim's surprised call. He couldn't…He had to think.

Sera. Here. Christ.

Chapter Nineteen

SITTING ON THE BED in the room that had been assigned to her, Sera stared at the closed door. On the other side stood Waithe Hall and the celebrations of the upcoming marriage of Lydia Torrence and the Earl of Roxwaithe.

On the other side stood her chance with Stephen.

Exhaling, she looked down. She'd arrived at Waithe Hall late yesterday afternoon, after the sun had set and as darkness began to mar the path. A mix up with her trunks at the previous lodging had delayed her departure and, though it had been foolish to set out with the knowledge it could have been both dark *and* snowing during her journey, she'd not wanted to delay her arrival any longer. Her stomach already churned too much, and she'd bitten her nails to the quick. She wanted one part of this over, and being so close to its completion, she'd wanted no part of a delay. Arriving so late had meant she'd been greeted by servants rather than her hosts and, to be perfectly honest, she'd preferred the servants to Lydia Torrence. She had been irritable, overwrought and travel-weary, and in no frame of mind to deal with Lydia and the mess she had made. A maid had led her to her room, and she'd sent Delphine to the kitchens to request a tray be brought to her room.

And thus she had seen no one and spoken to no one and now she sat here, staring at a door and reluctant to leave her room.

Closing her eyes, she swallowed. *Say it true, Sera.* She was *scared* to leave her room.

How utterly ridiculous. She had never in her life been apprehensive to enter society. Her presence was desired at gatherings from Carlisle to Dover and all the places in between.

She squared her shoulders. She couldn't stay here in her room forever. She was Seraphina Waller-Mitchell. She could do anything she set her mind to and she would not let apprehension get the better of her.

So resolved, she swept from her room.

Waithe Hall was cavernous, and she found herself turned around four times before she finally made it to the dining room for breakfast. The halls were decorated with sprigs of holly and ivy, strung cranberries, and boughs of mistletoe. She'd never in her life seen such a saturation of decorations, especially in what had to be infrequently used halls. Usually her Christmases were spent in London, attending whatever society gatherings remained. Some decorated but most did not, and never in such abundance.

Outside the dining room, she hesitated. She could not recall she had ever been alone at a house party. Always she'd been flanked by Maria and Elizabeth, and she felt horribly exposed to be by herself.

Again, she squared her shoulders. She was Seraphina Waller-Mitchell. She could do this. Chanting it over and over in her head, she entered the room.

A long rectangular table burdened with piping hot food occupied the room, half of the seats filled. Perhaps the other guests were still to arrive. At the end of the table, the Earl of Roxwaithe bent his head to Lydia's bright red one, Lydia's shoulders shaking with mirth. They looked…happy. Sera couldn't ever remember feeling as happy as they looked. What would that feel like? What would it be like to have that connection with someone, to laugh and talk and…hold your hand, as the earl now did with Lydia?

Lydia looked up and caught Sera staring at them. Her smile dipped before becoming a brittle thing. The earl noticed and followed her gaze, his brows drawing as he spied her.

She lifted her chin. She would not be intimidated.

Earl Wainwright sat to the left of Lord Roxwaithe, carefully spreading butter on his lady's toast. The countess watched him with amusement, her hand cradling her gently rounded belly.

A few empty seats from them sat Lord Maxim Farlisle, his large frame tense and uneasy. Alexandra Torrence sat beside him conversing with her younger brother, but her hand was tightly clutched in Lord Maxim's.

Sera exhaled in annoyance. Alexandra *Farlisle* now. It should be easy to remember the Torrence sisters' new names. They would soon again share the same one.

To the right of Lydia and with her arms crossed, Lady Violet Crafers scowled at her.

Sera lifted her chin. She didn't care what Violet Crafers thought of her.

The Duke of Meacham appeared at Violet's side, holding a steaming teacup as he sat beside her. Her scowl shifted from Sera to him as he spoke with a ridiculous level of cheeriness, her scowl deepening with every word.

The Marquis of Demartine conversed with the Earl of Ashburton, the younger lord gesticulating wildly with the piece of toast in his grasp. The Marchioness sat with her eldest son, Viscount Raison, and his fiancée—his sisters had seen fit to marry before him, though of the three he was the one who had been affianced the longest.

The Marchioness spied her loitering awkwardly in the entrance and, smiling warmly, rose to greet her. "Ah, Lady Seraphina. We are delighted you are come. It seems we are thin on the ground today, so it is well Lord Demartine and I chose to break our fast here at Waithe Hall. Many, I believe, have chosen to take a tray in their rooms after their long journey."

"I—" She couldn't think of an adequate response. Her gaze whipped again around the table. This was it? This was the sum total of the guests? This was supposed to be a crush. A true house party, with dozens upon dozens of guests. It was not to be family and friends...and Sera, who was neither.

Panic suffused her. She wanted to turn on her heel, to run, to call for her carriage and leave. She couldn't— This wasn't—

Lady Demartine, it seemed, saw her panic. "Sit beside me, dear, and break your fast," she said gently.

Jerkily, she did so. A plate appeared before her and she stared at it. She had not looked at him yet. But now, taking a breath and stealing herself, she did.

Stephen sat further down the table, an empty seat on both sides. He looked the same: tousled blond hair, clothes slightly out of fashion, aloof. He focussed on the plate before him, conversing with no one. And it seemed to her he was still so alone. Even here, in the midst of his family.

A pain began in her chest, a dull throb.

Her gaze devoured him greedily. It wasn't until now, until she saw him again, that she realised how much she'd noticed the lack of him. The way she could sometimes get the corner of his mouth to kick up. The way that sardonic dark gaze would focus on her and her only, until she was aware of no other person around them. The way that, with him, she didn't feel alone.

Next to her, Lady Demartine said, "Shall we skate today? It seemed the ice thickened overnight."

"Did you check, then, Mama?" Viscount Raison teased.

"Hush, child." The countess's blue eyes turned to her. "Lady Seraphina? Would you enjoy skating?"

"I—" Horribly, terribly, her mind went blank. "Yes?"

"Excellent. Well then, you and I shall skate. And if others see fit to join us, they are most welcome."

"Mama, you fool no one," Lady Alexandra said.

"I am not attempting to fool anyone, Alexandra. I am merely stating my intention."

"And we are all to attend skating or—"

"You hush, too. You will give Lady Seraphina a terrible impression of me."

Alexandra grinned. "Why are you and Papa here, Mama? You have a perfectly good estate not half an hour's walk from here."

"We are here to support our daughters and their husbands, and to partake of the truly excellent food. Don't tell Mrs Murdoch, but I do so prefer the breakfasts at Waithe Hall."

"Not tell your cook you dislike her food? What will you give me?"

"I will not bat you upside the head, you ungrateful child," Lady Demartine said cheerfully.

Alexandra merely grinned.

Sera switched her gaze between them. Was this what family breakfasts were like? This banter?

Turning her gaze from Lady Demartine and her grinning daughter, Sera looked across the table.

Stephen stared at her, unsmiling.

Her heart froze. She could not tear her gaze from his and, as always, she forgot there were others in the room. She was consumed with his dark gaze, his face thinner than she remembered, his expression more stern. She wanted to smooth his brow, wanted to tease a quirk of the lips from him. He didn't smile, not really, but she could sometimes...

"So it is settled. We will skate. Excellent." Lady Demartine turned to her. "Lady Seraphina, you must tell me of your journey here. I hope it wasn't too treacherous."

Tearing her gaze from Stephen, she answered Lady Demartine's question, and the next, and the next. And all the while she felt Stephen's gaze burn into her, even as they finished their meal, even as they left the dining room. Even as she went back to her room, as she changed her gown, as she made her way to the frozen lake.

Even as she desperately tried to think of what she could possibly say to him.

Chapter Twenty

STEPHEN PUSHED HIMSELF HARDER, the burn in his thighs screaming as he streaked across the ice. Without his regime of regular exercise, his muscles had seized somewhat. As there was nowhere at Waithe Hall he could swim without freezing his ballocks off, and though the running and stretching he was able to do inside Waithe Hall kept the worst of it at bay, he still felt it every morning when he woke. Perhaps it was he could take up ice skating in the interim. It didn't seem to be as effective as swimming, but it might be it would be better than nothing.

Skidding to a stop, he massaged the ache in his thigh. This side of the lake was deserted, the rest of the party gathered in the distance. The lake at Waithe Hall was vast, and the canopy sheltering refreshments was a good while from where he now stood. In the distance, he could see the rest of the party skating in front of the canopy or on the banks taking refreshments, huddled in their cloaks and furs.

More than a few stared at Maxim, and had since they'd arrived at the lake. He'd ignored them though, and Stephen pictured the concentration on his brother's face as he found again his skating feet, Alexandra skating circles around him as she smiled and called encouragement.

Even from here, Stephen could see his elder brother still had his arms wrapped around his fiancée. Oliver had claimed he was keeping Lydia steady as she skated, and she had giggled and grinned as she clung to his forearms, as if she hadn't been skating on their lake since she was a toddler.

He couldn't help himself. Even as he told himself he shouldn't, he sought her out. Sera stood by herself, her brow creased and her stance unsteady. It had been obvious Lydia's pretence was her truth—she had no idea how to skate.

Deliberately, Stephen turned his back. It was no concern of his if she could not keep her feet and he was not, in the slightest, tempted to hold her as his elder brother did Lydia.

"Bloody hell, Farlisle, why did you bloody come all the bloody way over here?" Ash huffed as he scrambled to a stop next to Stephen, his face red.

He stopped massaging his thigh. "You didn't have to follow."

"True." Bent over with hands braced on his thighs, Ash took great gulps of air. "Is it all the football? Is that why you aren't dying?"

Ignoring him, Stephen skated in a circle around him. Now that his muscles were warm, he'd best maintain it.

"Jesus, how do you do that?"

Stephen shrugged.

Taking one last breath, Ash straightened. "So, who is it you're avoiding? The older brother, the younger, or Lady Seraphina?"

Stephen stumbled. "What?"

"Can't be the younger brother. Lord Maxim has been gone too long for you to form some sort of resentment to him. The earl is too wrapped up in his future bride to have done anything to truly vex you. Therefore…" Ash raised a brow.

"I don't know what you're thinking, Ash, but you are wrong."

Deliberately Ash glanced at the party in the distance and then back at Stephen.

"I'm not avoiding her."

"Clearly." Ash regarded him steadily. "What did Sutton say?"

Sutton? What did he have to do with anything? "When?"

"When you spoke about the wager."

Sharp pain twinged in his chest. "We didn't speak about the wager. I sent him a note, I conceded, I paid my forfeit, and it is done."

"She doesn't think it done."

Stephen managed to stop himself from glancing at her again, but the fact he could picture her so clearly gave lie to his claim he hadn't noticed her. Sera stood by herself, apart from the rest of the guests, her expression mulish as if it caused her no concern that she was alone. She had been the same at breakfast, her expression falling when she realised most of the guests had kept to their rooms. She had held her head high as she'd sat at the table, and when she'd sent an entreating glance his way, it had taken everything inside him not to respond.

"You know she's here for you, don't you?" Ash said.

Of course he knew. Why else would she be here? He rubbed at his chest.

"What happened, Farlisle?"

"Nothing," he said shortly. "Nothing happened. I lost the wager. There is nothing more to speak of."

"I would believe you, but you've been glancing at her this entire time, just as she's been seeking you out. Maybe you should speak with her."

"And maybe you should mind your goddamn business!"

The shouted words hung between them. Stunned, Ash stared at him. With a muttered curse, Stephen hung his head.

"Farlisle, you clearly feel something for her, as she does you. She is here, within reach. I would not recommend leaving such things unsaid."

Stephen glanced up sharply. Ash wore a peculiar expression. "Ash?"

His friend shook himself. "Talk with her. At the very least, you will wonder no more."

"How do you know I wonder?"

"Because we always do."

Stephen shook his head. "There is nothing to talk about. We are done."

"Farlisle—"

"I'm going back to the hall. Enjoy the skating, Ash." Ignoring his friend's protests, he took off.

He took care to skate as far from the others as possible, but his boots were with the others under the canopy. He kept his gaze down as he stepped off the ice, and he managed to get his skates off and one boot half on before someone approached.

"Stephen?" Sera asked hesitantly.

He swallowed. Christ. He'd missed her voice. Keeping his head down, he focussed on pulling his boot the rest of the way.

"You looked well on the ice."

Still he pretended he ignored her, even as a voice inside him screamed to look at her, to drink her in. His chest felt as if squeezed by iron bands, and it became difficult to breathe.

"You were so fast, but I thought perhaps the action might have tugged at your muscle, as you looked as if—"

"Lady Seraphina, was there a point to this?" he interrupted, the bands around his chest tightening.

She fell silent. "No."

"Then we are done." He stood. He dared not look at her. "Good day."

Between them, awful silence. Christ, he wanted to leave, he wanted to run, he wanted away from her. So much built inside him, emotions he didn't want to feel, and she was the cause of all of it. She would make him feel all of it. If he stayed here, if he let her speak, he wouldn't be able to keep it all inside. He would... Maxim... Harbor...

"Good day," she finally said.

Relief cascaded through him. With a sharp nod, he turned on his heel and strode to the house, away from the lake, away from her. The tension, though, that remained, coiled tight inside him, and it didn't matter where he went, what he did, it was still there. But, if he was away from her, he could pretend it didn't exist. No. No, it *didn't* exist...and if he avoided her, he would never have to believe otherwise.

Chapter Twenty One

From the best vantage of the drawing room, Sera watched the other ladies. They laughed and gossiped, and chief among the topics were the ceremony tomorrow, the celebration after, and how in love the bride and groom were. In the centre of this gossip and laughter sat a beaming Lydia Torrence, her sister at her side.

The gentlemen of the party had departed after dinner to smoke cigars, drink brandy, and no doubt indulge in gossip of their own. Stephen had been amongst them, though she'd noticed how he'd held himself separate. Only when his friend the Earl of Ashburton had jogged after him had another person stood by his side.

All through dinner she had watched Stephen, and how he studiously avoided her gaze. She'd barely heard the conversation of those around her, her brow creased as she contemplated how best to get him to look at her. The dinner had ended without her determining a way to do so, and he'd disappeared with the other gentlemen before she could at the very least speak with him again.

After their interaction at the frozen lake, she'd had to re-examine her strategy. It appeared the closeness they'd shared prior to...well, *prior* had dissipated. He would not look at her then, either, and he'd made his way from her as swiftly as he could. She'd spent the rest of the afternoon plotting a new course of action, but that too had failed. She squared her shoulders. No matter. This house party was to last at least another six days. She had ample opportunity.

Alexandra stood, her smile brilliant as she spoke. From here, Sera could not hear what she said, but Lydia broke out in a similar grin, laughing as her sister departed.

Sera stared at Lydia. She'd known the girl for so long, and had been at odds with her for almost all that time. She'd thought she'd been right, to propose to Stephen they use what she'd seen to blackmail his brother. She'd thought she'd been right, to prove to Lydia her hopes regarding the earl were ridiculous.

Perhaps she had not been right. Perhaps, as Charuni had said, she could have been a little kinder.

Abruptly, she made a decision.

Lydia's happiness faded as she noted Sera's approach. It wouldn't fade Sera's determination, however. "May I speak with you?"

"I suppose," Lydia said.

Ignoring the unenthusiastic response, Sera seated herself. "You did what you said you would."

"And what is that?"

"You will marry the earl."

Lydia stiffened.

"I am in awe of your perseverance. Well done."

"I do not enjoy your snide comments," Lydia said flatly.

Sera blinked. She did not mean— "I am not being snide."

Lydia laughed shortly. "I do not know why you have come to Waithe Hall. You were surely aware I sent the invitation in jest. You were never intended to be in attendance."

Sera told herself she imagined the hurt Lydia's words caused. She lifted her chin. "But you did send an invitation and I accepted. I now wish to offer my congratulations and felicitations on a happy marriage."

Lydia stared at her. "Every word out of your mouth sounds a curse."

Frustration made her words short. "I mean it true."

"Yes. For you are well known for your warmth and amiability."

This was not proceeding as she'd intended. She did not wish for Lydia's smile to have disappeared. She did not wish her words to have been taken not as she had intended. Is this the reaction she had sown? Is this what years of protecting herself with a sharp tongue and unkind words had produced? She wanted to be different. Her sister had been right. She needed to be kind.

A torrent of emotion swelled inside her. "I am sorry," she

burst out. "I am sorry for every cruel thing I said, every cruel thing I did. I am sorry."

Lydia remained stone-faced. "Are you sorry for every cruel deed and word to just to me? Or to everyone?"

She closed her eyes. "I am sorry." For everything. For every comment made. For every tear she caused. For every moment where she needed to feel better than everyone, and for every moment when it didn't work. She was sorry for it all.

Lydia was silent a moment. "You mean it, don't you?"

Lips pressed together, Sera nodded sharply.

"I accept your apology."

Jerking her head around, she stared at Lydia in shock. Just like that? With no further comment or recrimination? "I didn't think it would matter if I told everyone I saw you and Lord Roxwaithe. In the orangery," she blurted.

Lydia blinked. "I beg your pardon?"

"When I saw you at that ball. When you and the earl were—" her cheeks burned— "embracing. It was clear you would soon wed, and if I threatened a little scandal, everyone would forget as soon as the vows were said. It wouldn't have mattered."

Lydia simply stared at her. "Why didn't you tell everyone?" she finally said.

Sera swallowed. "Stephen asked me not to."

Lydia sucked in a breath. "You mean that courtship was real? I had heard you and he were spending time together, but... You do mean Stephen Farlisle? The Stephen who is related to Oliver? That Stephen?" She was so shocked she didn't seem to realise she had referred to Lord Roxwaithe by his given name...or that Sera had done the same with Stephen.

"Yes. He... He needed funds and I thought— But it doesn't matter now."

Seemingly stuck, Lydia said, "You and Stephen—"

She was tired of concealing everything, of playing games. So, she said plainly, "We were attempting to win a wager, so we spent time together pretending we were courting, and then I...he..."

Thoughtfully, Lydia cocked her head. "That might be an explanation for why he has been so irritable."

Sera's heart leapt. "He's been irritable?"

Lydia's frown returned. "That is neither here nor there."

"No, I suppose it isn't." Hesitantly, Sera said, "Friends?"

Even as she uttered the word, she knew how absurd it sounded.

Lydia thought it over. "Probably not."

"You are correct. Not friends. However, not enemies either."

"Indifferent acquaintances?"

"We will nod at each other at gatherings. Perhaps even exchange civil words."

"I can live with that."

"So can I."

"Truly, I am sorry," Sera said.

Looking bemused, Lydia nodded.

"I wish you the best for your marriage, and a lifetime of joy."

"Thank you." Lydia shook her head. "It is so odd hearing you say such things."

"I feel odd saying them."

That startled a laugh from Lydia. "Perhaps it was wise to invite you to my wedding."

"Perhaps it was." Sera stood. "I shall leave you to receive the well wishes of others. You deserve it."

Fascinated, Lydia stared at her. "So, so odd."

Chapter Twenty Two

T HE NEXT MORNING, LYDIA Torrence married the Earl of Roxwaithe.

Taking a sip of her champagne, Sera watched those around her. All day they had celebrated and now night had fallen, the clock striking the eleventh hour not twenty minutes ago. Celebrations were winding to a close, Lydia and the earl had disappeared an hour ago, and other guests were slowly making their way to their own beds.

Across the room, Stephen stood with his back to the panelling of the wall beside drapes that fell from the high ceiling to the floor. He had not yet noticed her, concealed as she was behind a rather large plinth.

After the wedding ceremony had concluded, she'd attempted to approach him again and again, but each time he evaded her. The celebration had spilled throughout Waithe Hall, and in each room she had entered, it was not more than half an hour before he noticed her pursuit and disappeared. She didn't know how he managed it. One moment he'd be in plain view, and the next he was gone, nothing left but the chatter of other guests.

Now, over the top of her champagne glass, she narrowed her gaze. He would not escape her this time.

"You make your interest obvious."

Keeping her gaze trained on Stephen, she greeted the Earl of Ashburton. "Do I, my lord?"

Leaning casually on the plinth's edge, he grinned. "I believe you are driving Farlisle spare with your pursuit. It is a glory to behold."

"Is there a point to this, Lord Ashburton?"

"Not really. Just wanted to let you know I approve."

She risked a sidelong gland at him. "Oh, good, just what I was longing for. Your approval. Truly, I feel completely validated."

His grin brightened. "Perfect. You are absolutely perfect for him."

Her cheeks burned. "He doesn't seem to believe I am."

"He's just being Farlisle. Continue with your pursuit, Lady Seraphina. He's a prickly one, is Farlisle, and he likes to pretend he doesn't care."

"But he does," she said firmly.

Lord Ashburton nodded. "But he does."

"Tell me, do you know how he disappears from each room? I never see him enter or exit."

The earl crossed his arms over his chest. "I suspect it's the secret passages."

Surprise drew her to glance at him. "Secret passages?"

"The Hall is riddled with them. Always used to brag about how he and his brothers would run about in them." He shifted uncomfortably. "You know, before..."

"Before his brother disappeared," she said when he didn't continue. "How is he? Has he spoken to you of Lord Maxim's return?"

"I don't know. Farlisle won't talk about it. Won't talk about much of anything." He looked at her. "He might talk to you."

"He's doing his level best not to," she said tartly.

That grin reappeared. "I have faith in you, Lady Seraphina."

Across the room, Stephen glanced about him and then ducked behind the drapes beside him. She frowned. "I believe he's about to employ the use of one of these secret passages now."

Lord Ashburton saluted her. "Good luck."

A quick smile her response, she made her way across the room. None seemed inclined to impede her, talking amongst themselves and disregarding her presence. Reaching where Stephen had stood, she looked about her to make sure none glanced her way and then ducked behind the drapes.

It was not obvious, where the entrance to the secret passage was. Whoever had designed it had been clever about it, concealing the join almost imperceptibly. However, once one knew it was there, the faintest of lines between one panel and the next fairly screamed secret passage. It took her a little longer to discover the trigger, but soon the panel opened smoothly to reveal a darkened passage. Taking a breath, she stepped inside.

The panel closed behind her, but the path before her was dimly lit by cracks in the walls. Cautiously, she moved forward, holding her skirts off the floor as she picked her way through the passage. Stairs appeared before her and she climbed them, the murmurs of those she'd left behind becoming more distant with each step.

She wasn't sure how long she'd climbed before the stairs levelled out to a short corridor leading to a wall with a large circular handle displayed prominently. This must be the end of the passage. Taking hold of the handle, she twisted it. The wall slid open, displaying a room lit by moonlight. Cautiously, she entered as silently as she could, unsure what she would find.

Three small beds flanked the walls at opposites to each other, wooden chests at the end of each. A rocking horse stood off the side, a bookshelf filled with what could only be children's tales occupied one wall, and a tall basket filled with cricket bats, croquet mallets, and footballs. Two large windows punctuated the wall to her right and, standing in front of the one farthest from her, was Stephen.

The curtains opened, he stared out into the night, the light of the moon playing over his severe features. He looked troubled, and tired, and dear. So dear.

Softly, she said, "Stephen."

He tensed. Waiting was an agony before he finally turned, his expression neutral.

"Sera," he said.

Chapter Twenty Three

It had been a long day.

Rubbing the back of his neck, Stephen stared out the nursery window. Light from the ballroom spilled faint illumination though night shrouded the rest, the moon casting a faint outline of trees before fading into nothingness. All was calm and silent outside, and he wished like hell he were the same.

His mind churned, and he barely held the emotion roiling inside him in check. It had become worse as the day progressed, and he couldn't rightly say *why* he felt such.

The wedding ceremony had been relatively short, Oliver and Lydia incandescently happy to finally be wed, and Stephen had overheard more than one guest comment in horrified delight at how indecently early the newly-married couple had departed. Maxim and Alexandra hadn't been any more circumspect, their hands laced and their heads bent before they too departed well before the celebrations were winding to a close.

Stephen had stood by himself, barely holding himself in check.

It hadn't helped Sera had pursued him with all the determination of which he knew her capable. He'd finally resorted to disappearing into the secret passage to the nursery, hoping the room of his youth would offer him again the comfort he'd always gleaned from it. Here, he and Oliver had created the code they'd used to write each other messages, recorded in a notebook they'd hidden amongst the books in the bookcase, code he still faintly remembered. Here, Maxim and he had thrown balls into a basket, keeping a score that had rolled over years. Here, he'd been with his brothers, and he'd been happy.

"Stephen."

He tensed. He should have known. Exhaling, he turned. "Sera."

She came forward and moonlight lit her face. She looked beautiful, but then she always looked beautiful to him. A gold band separated the skirt of her deep blue gown from the bodice, and he tried really hard not to notice the swell of her breasts above the low-cut neckline. Her dark hair was swept up in a complicated pile of curls, but her grey cat's eyes were solemn, her rose-pink lips unsmiling.

Christ, he'd missed her.

Setting his jaw, he steeled himself. "What are you doing here?"

"I am here for the earl and new countess's wedding."

He smiled without humour. Ah, pedantism. Lovely. "As are we all. Let me rephrase. Why are you here, before me, in the nursery of Waithe Hall that, as last I checked, was not visited by guests to the Earl of Roxwaithe's ancestral home?'

She blinked. "Ah. Well. I followed you."

"The truth of the matter. Delightful."

Her brows drew. Did he detect a hint of annoyance? Good. Maybe she would leave him alone. "You wouldn't talk to me. Every time I entered a room, you would leave."

In a move he'd seen Sutton perform a hundred times, and he knew to be particularly irritating, he lifted his brow. "Did that not tell you that perhaps I didn't *want* to talk with you?"

A full scowl. "Of course it told me that, but you are incorrect in that desire. We have to talk."

He gave a short laugh. "And we will do as you decree, with no consideration for my wants at all." His gaze slid past her. "You should not have followed me."

"Because you do not wish to speak with me."

"That is one reason," he agreed. "Another is you could have been lost, or hurt, or trapped within the walls of Waithe Hall, and none would have known."

She blinked. "I followed you."

"Yes, but I know my way around the passages," he said mildly. "I would not have stumbled over an unexpected staircase, or walked straight into an unknown break in the floor. I would not have jagged myself on any one of the broken beams and shafts, or turned the wrong way and found myself wandering for hours."

"None of that happened to me."

"But it could have."

She lifted her chin mulishly. "But it didn't."

Abruptly weary, he ran a hand over his face. "What are you doing here, Sera?"

"I told you. We need to talk. I have tried, over and again, to do so since my arrival. I need to...Stephen, I need to apologise."

A burn started in his chest. "There is no need," he said dismissively.

"There is every need. I...I did not behave well." She shuddered through a breath. "I did not know you felt so strongly for your brother, but that is no excuse. I should not have suggested such a thing and I promise you, I am trying to be better. I know I can be cruel and unkind. I would never again put you in such a position, and I ask for your forgiveness that I ever did."

He stared at her. She regarded him back, hands linked, her grey eyes pleading.

Christ, what did he say to that? How could he tell her he had forgiven her long ago? How could he tell her he missed her, he wanted her? How could he tell her all that, and not fall apart? Because if he told her that, if he told her he'd forgiven her, she would see...she would see that while he was glad Maxim had returned... he resented that Harbor hadn't.

"I would have come to you sooner, but I...I tried, but I could not, Roxegate was not accepting guests because of...your brother."

He hardened himself, pushing aside the emotion as he'd done since his brother's return. "My brother... What?"

Clearly perplexed, she drew her brows. "Your brother, he...returned."

Fingers digging into his biceps, he queried, "And why did that stop you?"

"Because...Stephen, you must know I wanted to come, but I—" She fell silent.

"You..." he prompted. She set her jaw, and so he continued. "It has not stopped you from attending a wedding and house party when you know you are not welcome. It did not stop you from pursuing an audience with me which I clearly did not desire. Why would a little thing like my dead brother's return stop you?"

The crease between her brows deepened. "Stephen, is all well with you?"

His eyes burned, and he swallowed against the lump in his throat. "I am fine," he bit off.

She tilted her head. "You do not seem fine."

"Well, I am."

Stepping closer, she lifted her hand. He flinched away before she could touch him.

"Stephen..."

Shaking his head, he turned his back on her and gazed sightlessly out the window.

He heard her make a sound of frustration. "Stephen, you cannot do this to me. You cannot ignore me, and you certainly can't ignore what you feel. You can turn your back on me as much as you like, but I shan't go away. I will not leave you. I will never leave you."

"What do you know of staying, when both your parents abandoned you?"

She drew in a sharp breath.

He closed his eyes. He shouldn't have said that. He didn't mean it, and he'd hurt her. Christ, he never wanted to hurt her, but...he... he couldn't...

"That was unfair," she said quietly.

His lips twisted into a mockery of a smile. Christ. Didn't he know it.

"You can't get rid of me, no matter what you say. You see, I know something of using anger and hurt as a weapon."

She sounded sad, and a little lost. He clenched his teeth.

Arms crept around him, and he felt her lay her cheek on his shoulder, her front against his back. "It must have been hard."

His jaw ached. Her hands were warm on his chest.

"When he came back. It must have been devastating."

He took a rasping breath, and when he covered her hands with his, they shook. Bowing his head, he said hoarsely, "He came back, Sera. He came back and he wasn't dead and I...I didn't know how to feel."

She said nothing further, but her arms tightened around him.

His cheeks were wet. "Because if he came back...If Maxim came back, then why couldn't Harbor?" Emotion, so long suppressed, exploded. "And what did that make me, Sera? Why wasn't I ecstatic my brother had returned, when all I could think of was Harbor. Harbor was still dead. He would never return and it wasn't fair. It wasn't fair we were given this miracle and not another, and how could I think this about my brother? How could I be resentful? *How?*"

He stared out the window but he saw Maxim, standing in the doorway to Oliver's study at Roxegate House, his hand held tightly in Alexandra's. "He came back, Sera," he said hoarsely.

"I know."

With a harsh sob, he turned in her arms, burying his head in her shoulder. She held him, making soothing noises as he shuddered in her embrace.

Slowly, the maelstrom receded, and he felt...lighter. Taking a breath, he lifted his head. Sera looked back at him, her own eyes damp, and all he could see was her. He cupped her face. She searched his.

Slowly, he lowered his mouth to hers.

Her lips opened to his, so sweetly, and he poured everything into this kiss, all his gratitude and his thanks, his desire, how much he missed her, how he'd longed for her. All this time, he'd needed her and he hadn't even known it, and now she'd forced herself back into his life, and he couldn't be more grateful that she'd done so. That she'd made him see. That she was here, with him, and she wanted him.

They broke apart.

He stared into her eyes and she stared back.

"This isn't because of emotion," he said.

She blinked. "Pardon?"

"Why I kissed you. It isn't because of Maxim, or Harbor. It's because of you."

Her brow creased. "All...right."

"It's because I want you." He kissed her brow. "I desire you." He kissed the other. "I need you." He kissed below her ear.

She shuddered. "I did not think otherwise."

"But I want you to know." He pulled back. "I am not losing myself in you. This is not because of grief."

She smoothed his hair at his temple. "I believe you."

"Good," he said simply. And then he kissed her.

Chapter Twenty Four

Sera hadn't known what to expect when she finally made Stephen talk to her, but it hadn't been this. It hadn't been an outpouring of emotion, of devastation and loss, and then for him to kiss her as if he couldn't breathe without her.

Not that she was complaining.

Tangling her fingers in his hair, she opened herself to his kiss. His tongue swept inside to tangle with hers, and she tasted salt on his lips.

Her heart ached for him, for all he'd endured. And it ached for her, that she hadn't been able to comfort him. But she was now and, God willing, she always would be.

Pulling back, she swept her thumbs over his damp cheeks, and he smiled at her.

She sucked in her breath. Lord. That smile.

His gaze darkened, and he drew her to him once more. This time, his kiss was like fire. He kissed her, and she never wanted him to stop, she wanted to be with him like this always. She had missed him so much. Now, they were together, and she could think of nothing but being closer to him.

Pulling his mouth from hers, he trailed kisses down her jaw, his hands tight on her hips. He licked her neck and she shuddered. Desperately, she pulled at his coat and he struggled out of it, cursing as it caught on his arms. Attacking his cravat only made it tighter, and she moaned in dismay, wanting to taste his skin only to be stymied by fabric.

With a growl, Stephen ripped the knot open, and she unwound the fabric as he assaulted the buttons on her back. Her dress gaped and then fell, exposing her stays and chemise, and he curled his hand around her neck, his thumb forcing her chin up. She met his gaze with challenge and he took her mouth, his other hand sliding over her shoulder to cup her breast through her stays. Her nipple hardened as he pushed her flesh up, his fingers shaping her as he liked. She moaned his name, feeling the tug of it deep in her belly, her core wet and aching. He pushed his hips into her and he was hard against her stomach, his mouth savage as he devoured her with his mouth.

The edge of a bed pressed into the back of her thighs and then she tumbled, landing in a swirl of fabric. He followed her down, dropping kisses over her collarbone, her breasts, and she arched into him, wanting more. Wanting everything.

Straddling her thighs, he reared above her, all lean strength and pale skin. Muscle rounded his shoulders and corded through his arms, the bulging of his biceps revealed as he tugged his shirt over his head. A curl of blond fell over his forehead, and he stared down at her with intense dark eyes, his face a mask of desire. He was so pretty, and he could have any one of a hundred women.

Unaccustomed doubt crept in. Perhaps they shouldn't do this. She had no desire for him to feel trapped, or for him to believe she'd planned to trap him. What if he thought she had planned to trap him? "Do you want this?"

He paused, his chest expanding with each harsh breath even as his mouth turned up at the corner. "I should be asking you that."

The white-hot passion of moments ago cooled a little, and she found herself scowling. "Why?"

"Because I have less to lose."

"I have nothing to lose," she argued.

"Just your maidenhead," he retorted. Then he blinked. "Do you have a maidenhead to lose?"

She hit him.

He grinned. "I'll take that as a yes." His expression softened. "Thank you for telling me. I needed to know, to make this good for you."

She lifted her chin. "See that you do," she said, and her voice only slightly wobbled.

Still grinning, he leant down to capture her lips with his. "Sit up."

She did as he bade and he tugged at the laces of her stays, removing the garment with distressing ease. "I don't want to think about why you're so good at that," she said tartly.

"I used to be quite well-versed in bed sport," he replied nonchalantly.

He knew much and she knew little. "Wonderful," she muttered.

"I used to be, Sera." Capturing her chin, he laid an almost chaste kiss on her lips. "But now I want no one but you."

"Oh. Well." Flustered, she waved a hand. "I suppose then you may continue."

A faint smile on his face, he raised a brow. "Oh I may, may I?"

Joy burst within her. This man, this beautiful man. This man who understood her, who valued her, who knew she concealed great emotion with imperiousness. "You may."

Smiling, his lips brushed over her collarbone, and then lower. His mouth closed over her breast, and fire streaked inside her as he worried her nipple with his tongue and his teeth. He pulled back to admire his handiwork, her flesh reddened and distended. She arched for him, her breasts aching, and he lowered his head again, this time to worship her other breast, his fingers plucking at the one he'd abandoned as she thrashed beneath him, the sensations almost too much.

Rising again, he stared at her, his gaze running over her face, her breasts, her belly, and then he pushed his breeches down, his drawers hanging low on his hips. A tan line bisected his abdomen below his navel, separating the tanned flesh of his chest and arms from the paler skin of his hips. Her mouth watered as she imagined on his football pitch, his shirt off and his strong form exposed to the sun.

Leaning over her, he caged her in warmth and muscle as his thighs pushed hers apart, and she drew in her breath sharply as his hardness pressed against her. One hand travelled down her side and curled around the back of her thigh, pulling her knee against his hip. A gentle thrust pushed him against her core through her petticoats and his drawers, and she gasped, hot and wet and so desperate to have him inside. Frantically, she pushed at his drawers, cupping his firm buttocks to pull her closer, closer. He tugged at the ties at her waist and then he dragged her petticoats from her, and then her chemise, and then there was nothing between them. His touch drifted to her mound, through her curls, and she held her breath as he gently stroked the seam between her legs, feeling for himself how wet she was.

He pulled back. She urged him against her but he refused to move.

Dark eyes searched hers. "You haven't done this before?"

"What?" A frown touched her brow. "Haven't we already discussed this?"

"We did, but..." He looked...unhappy. "I don't want to hurt you."

"Well, you're going to," she said bluntly.

"Christ. I'm going to hurt you." He touched his forehead to hers. "How on earth do I do this?"

"Do you really need me to explain it to you? Because I will."

He didn't raise his head, but she saw the faintest of smiles.

"Stephen." She twined her fingers in the hair at the base of his skull. "Come inside me."

He closed his eyes, swallowed. Then, she felt him push inside her. She drew in her breath as he retreated and pushed again, a little deeper. It felt strange, and burned a little. He pushed further and further, and then he stilled, the whole of him inside her, his forehead against hers, his chest bellowing.

"Did I hurt you?" he ground out.

"Not really." She shifted beneath him. She felt full and heavy and he burned inside her and he was deep, so deep. "It feels...strange. Good, but strange."

He groaned. "Don't move. I haven't...it's been a while. Don't move."

She moved her hips, and he growled. Fascinated, she did it again.

"You're doing it on purpose, aren't you?"

"Maybe." She moved again, and then he hit something inside her that made her see stars. She gasped, her neck arching.

"There?" He pushed, and sensation streaked through her. "There, Sera?"

She couldn't speak, she was too full, too full of him, too full of pleasure.

"There," he said, and then he thrust again.

She couldn't think, she could only hold on to him as he built the pleasure inside her, driving her higher and higher.

He snarled, and then he pulled out of her. She wailed, wanting him back, but he flipped onto his back, hauling her over him, spreading her thighs wide as he brought her to straddle him.

He thrust up into her and she felt him so deep, so thick and deep inside her, and she slammed herself into his thrust, arching her back as his hands covered her breasts, moulding her flesh, pinching her nipples. Pleasure exploded inside her and she gave a soundless scream, barely hearing his harsh growl as his hands moved to her hips. He moved her as he wanted, thrusting up into her without rhythm, his lip curled as he grunted and moaned, wild in his lust, and then he came, his neck arched.

She collapsed on him, sucking in breath as his chest rose and fell beneath erratically, his hands still cupping her hips. He was still inside her, warm and full and hers.

Against his chest, she closed her eyes. The sound of his heart was strong and steady, and she felt the whisper of his lips against her temple as she drifted into sleep.

Chapter Twenty Five

FAINT LIGHT SHONE THROUGH the nursery window, painting the tangled bed clothes with pale fingers. Soon, the sun would rise in earnest, and brightness would chase the dim from the nursery.

Watching the light's progress, Stephen trailed his hand up and down Sera's arm. Her breath was light and even over his bare chest. She wore her chemise, the skirt bunched up around her thighs and one sleeveless strap falling off her shoulder. A smile touched his mouth as he recalled her, her cheeks a fiery red as she'd slipped the chemise over her head even as she insisted it wasn't a concession to modesty. He'd wisely kept his mouth shut, his smirk all he needed to inform her he saw right though her protests. She could be so bold, and yet she blushed to sleep naked beside him, even after he had seen for himself how beautiful she was. He loved that about her. He loved all her contradictions, and now he would get to enjoy her contradictions for the rest of his life. It hadn't been his first thought after they had made love, but he knew it now. They must marry.

Her skin was smooth, warm and lovely under his fingers. They would be missed. They had both fallen asleep, and night had turned slowly to day. It was still early enough that not even the servants would have risen as yet, and it could well be they would both make it back to their respective beds without anyone the wiser. The problem was, he never wanted to move.

Calmness settled inside him. There was no choice. It had been decided the moment he'd turned and seen her. She would be his, and he would be hers, and that's all there was to it. He would have to tell Oliver. As head of the family, he was going to have to know.

His fingers paused. He needed a plan for how to approach this. He had to get Oliver to agree, but that was for later. For now, he had Sera in his arms and daybreak was upon them.

Tracing his fingers over her temple, he curled her hair behind her ear. "Sera," he said softly.

She didn't stir.

"Sera."

Nothing.

Leaning closer, he brushed his lips over her cheek "Sera."

"Hmm?" Her lashes fluttered and hazy grey eyes focussed on him. She smiled sleepily. "Stephen."

His heart clenched. Brushing his lips over hers, he tried to convey all he felt, all the desire, all the happiness, all the joy.

That sleepy smile was still on her face when he pulled back. "Good morning," she said softly.

"Good morning." Heart full, he watched as she sat up. The bed clothes fell about her waist and, though she'd put her chemise back on, it was so sheer he could see her nipples. His mouth watered.

Her gaze roamed over him, smile fading as lazy heat filled her eyes. "You are not wearing a shirt."

"No." He stretched his arms over his head. Her eyes darkened, tracking his movements avidly. He concealed his smirk. "Like something you see?"

Her gaze darted to his, and he could conceal his smirk no longer. With an exclamation, she hit him on his bicep. Then, her touch gentled as she traced his bare skin, tracing the muscle. He swallowed hard, his skin tingling everywhere her fingers skimmed. "You didn't let me explore you."

"Well then." Clearing his throat, he spread his arms wide. "Have at it."

With a superior look, she pulled the sheet to his waist. Her gaze roved over him and he responded, his cock twitching under the covers. She looked fascinated, as if his body was the most interesting thing she'd ever seen.

He could tell the exact moment she found the first scar.

Her fingers traced the past twisted into his flesh, the scar tissue bumpy. She made a sound of distress.

He wiped a tear from her cheek. "I thought you wanted to explore me."

She swallowed, and raised her tremulous gaze.

"It doesn't hurt so much anymore," he told her.

"But it still does?"

Reluctantly, he nodded. "Dr. Griffiths thinks it always will, and he's not been wrong so far. There are things I can do, though, exercises and the like. It's why I play football, and why I swim in the heath, and I undertake lifting weights, and stretch my muscles, and—"

She placed a finger over his lips, silencing him.

"I overreacted, you know," he said against her finger.

Her brows drew. "Pardon?"

"At the ball. To your proposal about Oliver and Lydia. I overreacted."

"Oh." She cleared her throat. "It was perhaps not the best plan."

"Perhaps not, but I did not react well. I should have called on you the next day. I should have...but then..." He rubbed a hand over his face.

"Your brother returned."

Hand still over his eyes, he nodded. "Maxim returned."

She was silent a moment. "Do you wish to speak of it?"

"Not particularly." Lowering his hand, he exhaled. "I don't know how I was supposed to feel."

"However you felt, I suppose."

"Not especially helpful, Sera."

"I have never had a dead brother return. I find I am quite unable to imagine what it would be like." She cocked her head. "I have been presented with an unknown sister, in fact, a whole raft of siblings I had no knowledge of. Do you believe it comparable?"

The corner of his mouth lifted. "Maybe."

"Well then, I declare myself an expert and posit to you your reaction was exactly appropriate and you must worry yourself about it no further." She nodded decisively.

He could not stop his smile. She looked so very determined, and so serious, and he could not be happier she was here with him. "What do you think about my feeling resentful Harbor did not also walk through the door?"

"Well, for one, I do not believe Roxegate House would have been his first port of call after returning. Second of all, it stands to reason."

"Why?"

"You did not just lose one brother—I am not wrong in supposing Lord Harbor was as a brother to you?"

Slowly, he shook his head.

She nodded to herself. "As I thought. You lost Lord Maxim, and then you lost Lord Harbor. It must have been devastating, Stephen. *You* must have been devastated. To have Lord Maxim return, against all reason and nothing short of a miracle, I should think it would be natural to wish the other loss undone. To wish for Lord Harbor's return. And, with the realisation he wouldn't, all the grief you felt at his passing would have come flooding back." She placed a hand on his cheek. "I would think such a reaction as yours wholly appropriate."

Eyes burning, he stared at her. Christ. Christ.

Gathering her to him, he kissed her, and in his kiss was gratitude and thanks and how the bloody hell did he ever get so fortunate as to win her regard?

Pulling back, she settled her hands on his shoulders. "By the bye, I forgive you," she said magnanimously.

He was confused only a moment before his lips twitched. "You forgive me for you having a stupid idea and me being upset about it?"

"Precisely."

He burst out laughing.

She looked at him in wonder.

"What?" he asked self-consciously.

"I don't think I've ever heard you laugh quite like that before."

"Surely not."

She shook her head, and her dark hair spilled over her shoulder. "I don't think I have."

"I shall ensure you hear it often in the future."

"Future?" she said, her eyes wide.

"I shall have to talk with Oliver."

"Stephen." She took his hand between hers, and he curled into her touch. "We are to have a future?"

He ducked his head. "Of course," he said gruffly. "We have no choice."

She stilled. "Of course," she repeated.

Why did he feel as if something had been lost? Brusquely, he continued, ignoring the feeling of unease. "I shall discuss with Oliver, and then we shall make arrangements. Perhaps we will to Gretna Green, though it will be just as simple to make arrangements here."

She said nothing.

"Sera?" he said.

A shadow passed over her eyes. "What sort of arrangements?"

"Well, we shall marry," he said awkwardly. Ignoring the trepidation in his gut, he powered through. "We have no choice, we shall have to marry. Oliver cannot protest, and neither can Lydia. Lady Demartine may be disappointed at my actions, but she won't voice concern either. There is nothing else for it but we must be wed. So, you see, none shall object."

She stared at him.

He shifted uncomfortably, a flush heating his skin. "Sera?"

She took forever to respond. "Talk with Oliver," she finally said.

He let out the breath he didn't realise he held. "Before breakfast, if I can help it."

Turning her cheek, she nodded. "Is there a way to my room from the nursery? A secret passage?"

"Yes. Of course." Again, that feeling of unease. "Shall I help you dress?"

Cheek still turned, she nodded. "Please."

He helped her dress in silence, and then he threw on his shirt and breeches. Holding the rest of his clothes, he placed a hand at her back as he kissed her forehead. "All will be well."

Avoiding his gaze, she nodded.

He led her through the passage to her room, avoiding discovery on the short walk through the hall that wasn't covered by the passage.

"I will see you at breakfast," he said, and again she nodded before disappearing into her room.

Chapter Twenty Six

STEPHEN WAS NOT AT breakfast.

Her untouched toast growing cold, Sera stared out the window, seeing nothing beyond the blanket of white. Around her, others enjoyed their breakfast, talking and laughing and discussing the wedding and celebrations of the previous evening, but she could not bring herself to join any of the conversations flowing around her. Instead, she stared out the window and let her toast grow cold.

She should be happy. She had spoken with Stephen and, what's more, he had spoken with her. He had let her comfort him, and then...then they had made love. She knew she was supposed to have refused him, was supposed to have guarded her chastity at all costs. But she had wanted him, and it had seemed natural to kiss him and touch him and allow him to touch her, and she could not regret something that had given her such pleasure. Waking up to his husky voice, his smile, had been even better.

And then he had told her he would 'make arrangements'.

Across the room, the Earl of Ashburton grinned at her. She did not know why. He had no notion what had happened last night, not unless he had seen Stephen this morning and Stephen had told him, but she had no fear of that. Stephen would tell no one—it was not his nature. More often than not, he remained silent and unsmiling, letting others talk around him, though she could sometimes steal a smile from him, and even more rarely a laugh.

Something burned sharp and deep in her chest.

Standing, she left her cold toast behind as she left the

breakfast room, not knowing her destination but knowing she could no longer be here in the room Stephen had promised he would attend. Other guests milled in the corridors, and she didn't want to be amongst them either, so she found herself returning to her room, lying on her bed with her hand laced over her stomach and staring at the canopy above.

Was it concern about gaining permission from his brother? The Earl of Roxwaithe most likely did not hold her in esteem. She had been cruel to his new wife, after all, and he from all her observations loved Lydia to the point of madness.

Her throat closed. What must that be like? To be loved so desperately?

She had apologised to Lydia, though, and what's more, she had meant it. Perhaps at first it would be awkward, but she was Seraphina Waller-Mitchell. If she wanted a thing, she would find a way to get it, and if she wanted Lydia Torrence—Lydia *Farlisle*—as her friend, then it would be so. They were to be sisters-in-law and, as such, would be in each other's company often. She would *make* it so Lydia liked her. She had made it that the Ton feared and admired her. This would be no different.

No. That was not why she was not happy.

Her hands tightened on each other. She hadn't known what to think when he'd stumbled though his plan to 'make arrangements'. She hadn't known if he wanted her to object, to claim it was unnecessary. She hadn't known if he'd wanted her to gush with gratitude, to extol fortune in having an honourable man make an offer of marriage to protect her reputation.

All she could think was her mother hadn't wanted her. Her father had created a whole other family and never told her at all. Stephen, it appeared, was no different—he wanted her, but only because his hand was forced by their unwise actions. But they hadn't been unwise to her. She had thought she had been expressing...love.

She'd looked at him looking at her, discomfort and uncertainty in his eyes, and she had no idea what he wanted her to say. In the end, she could only agree. They would have a good marriage. They would make it a good marriage, but it would not be what she wanted...what she hadn't known she'd wanted, until all possibility of it had been removed: To marry for love, and not just obligation.

Clearly, he did not feel the same.

She could, quite politely, refused him. She could, quite

politely, tell him she'd realised they did not suit and he needn't worry that he had compromised her. It was unlikely she was with child after one night, and even if she was there were ways to deal with an unwanted child.

She blanched. Never would she call her child unwanted, no matter the circumstances surrounding their birth. She knew what it was to be unwanted. However, this hypothetical child was just that. There was no reason to wed. None.

If she refused, though, if she told Stephen they did not suit, then she would not have him, and she wanted him. With every fibre of her being, she wanted him.

Sera smiled at the canopy without mirth. It appeared, when all was said and done, she was rather a pathetic sort. Who could have imagined that Seraphina Waller-Mitchell, the woman who had held the Ton at her feet, would settle for scraps from the man she loved?

A panel in the wall slid open. For some reason, she was not surprised when Stephen emerged, dusting at his shoulder and with cobwebs in his hair. Pushing herself up, she ran her gaze over him, the lean form she knew was corded with muscle, the chest she knew lightly dusted with golden hair. He was so handsome to her, so strong and sure. She loved his care for others, the way he wore his solemnity, the way he smiled for her. She loved that he let her see the broken pieces inside him, let her comfort him, and she loved that he did the same for her. She loved that he gave her himself.

But he did not love her.

He wore a frown as he approached the bed. "You were not in the breakfast room, and no one knew where you were. I've had the devil of a time trying to remember which passage led to your room, and almost set myself up for a supremely embarrassing conversation with Lady Parr. Thank Christ she wasn't in her room." Finally, he noticed her lack of response. "Sera?"

Lacing her hands in her lap, she regarded him impassively. "There is a passage to my room? Why did we not take it this morning?"

"It doesn't connect with the nursery." His large hand swept over his forearm, tugged at the sleeve of his jacket.

She remembered those hands, and how they had touched her. Her skin prickled, and a pressure started low in her belly. She pushed the memory away. "Why are you here?"

"I could not find Oliver, and then I remembered he and Lydia were wed yesterday, and they probably have not stopped fu—uh, well, you know," he finished lamely, his cheeks ablaze.

Such a sight should have made her laugh, or at least smile. She should have made a teasing remark at his almost-curse, or a ribald one, just to make him blush further. Instead, she tightened her hands in her lap. "So you have not spoken with him of your arrangements?"

He scowled. "Don't say it like that."

"It is how you described it."

"Be that as it may, do not say it such." Exhaling, he sat on the side of her bed and raked a hand through his disordered hair. "I am sorry. I did not think. It might be we will have to wait a day or so before I can speak with him."

She did not respond.

He frowned. "Sera?"

"Yes, of course. We will wait."

"Sera." He tipped her chin up with his thumb. "What is wrong?"

She slid her gaze past him. "Nothing."

"You cannot say such. Clearly, something is wrong."

"It is of little matter."

"It is of great matter. To me. Tell me."

"I am merely adjusting. My life has changed dramatically from yesterday to today. Yesterday, I did not have a fiancé and now, it appears I do. I am, as I said, adjusting."

He frowned. "Do you not want to marry me?"

She smiled bitterly. "Above all things, I want you. I want to be with you. I am reconciling myself to love you enough for both of us."

He started, his expression dumbfounded. "What?"

She didn't let herself look at him. "I will get over it, Stephen. Do not worry. Eventually, I shall be content. I am certain I can apply myself to it. Other women have, and I will not have them be better than I. I will be content with what you give me. I am determined it will be so."

"What?" he repeated.

Annoyance swirled. "Stephen, I have explained this is difficult for me. I understand my obligations. I understand you have sought permission from your brother and, though he is unavailable at present, you will be granted it. I will say my vows when required. I will be the best wife I can be. If it takes me a little time to reconcile myself to a marriage of obligation, duty, and I would hope a little affection, I beg you allow me that time."

"What do you mean, I don't love you?" he demanded.

She paused. "You have made no mention of it."

Staring at her, he made a choked sound and, rising from the bed, started to pace.

She watched him as he strode back and forth, back and forth.

Finally, he stilled. Shaking his head, he said almost to himself, "I've bollixed this up."

Pain seared through her. Oh, this was worse. This was so much worse. "You don't want to marry me at all?" she asked in a small voice.

He looked horrified. "No. Sera, of course not, I—" Sitting beside her once more, he took a breath. "I am not good at expressing my emotions."

A tiny thread of hope wound about her. "I have noticed that."

He gave her a small smile. "After last night, it became obvious we would need to wed."

Hope died. "Oh."

"No, I...again, I explain it badly." He exhaled in frustration. "I want to marry you because of what we did. And I want to marry you because I cannot imagine being happy without being your husband." He took a deep breath. "I want to marry you because I love you," he said in a rush.

Time stopped. "I beg your pardon?"

He set his jaw determinedly. "I love you."

"If you wouldn't mind repeating that again, I would be grateful."

At her polite tone, a reluctant smile teased the corner of his mouth. "I love you, Sera."

"Do you mean it?"

"Yes," he said softly.

Oh. Oh, that was...

Emotion swelled in her, too great to contain. She placed a hand over her mouth, trying to stop it, but emotion defeated her. It exploded, a harsh sob battering her as tears welled and spilled over.

His expression turned horrified, his hands reaching for her even before he obviously restrained himself, clearly uncertain if he should touch her. "God, Sera, I didn't mean to make you cry. I take it back."

"Don't you dare," she said fiercely. She took his hands, pulled his arms around her. "No one's ever chosen me. Never. You can't take it back. I won't let you take it back."

"I won't ever take it back." Wrapping her tight, he brushed his mouth against her temple. "You are never an obligation, Sera. You are never not my first choice. Always, forevermore, you are first for me. All my options have narrowed to one—you, and only you." He smiled ruefully. "That is what I should have said."

"That would have been better," she agreed.

He laughed, and then he kissed her. She fell backwards on the bed and he followed her, stretching himself over her and settling between her thighs. She draped her arms over him, dragging her fingers up and down his spine.

Looking into her eyes, he said, "Will you marry me?"

Joy bubbled inside her. "What about asking Oliver?"

He stroked her cheek. "He will allow it. I will accept nothing less."

Her cheeks hurt with her smile. "Then I will."

He smiled, one of pure joy. He bent his head. "We probably should go down to the breakfast room," he murmured against her lips.

"We won't be missed until at least luncheon." She rubbed her foot against his calf.

"Lady Seraphina, are you suggesting some sort of wickedness? Lady Asterd warned me about you."

"Well, then," she said, dragging his shirt from his breeches. "Far be it from me to disappoint her."

Epilogue

Roxegate
London, England
Twenty-four years later

Her cousin made a beautiful bride.

Miss Davina Farlisle watched as Holly and her new husband greeted their guests. Holly fairly beamed with happiness, while Hugh Delancy looked at his bride with a mixture of awe, pride, and love.

At the refreshment table, her other cousin stood with her husband. Charlotte and Nicholas had been wed not long after she and her cousins had turned nineteen while Holly had waited until they'd all had their twenty-first birthday before she'd wed.

Davina picked at her gown. She was being left behind. Her cousins had found the men they wanted to be with and it would no longer be the three of them. Now, her cousins had husbands and would be working on families of their own, while she would enter yet another season in another doomed attempt to attract a mate.

Her mother persisted, though it seemed it was completely pointless. Lady Seraphina Farlisle was a noted beauty and a triumph of the Ton, and she wanted nothing less for her children. Unfortunately, Davina was horribly tongue-tied around those she did not know, and her attractions were middling at best. She'd always relied on Charlotte and Holly to sparkle, and she would be a dull lump without their brilliance.

Across the room, her father congratulated her uncle on

his daughter's marriage. Lord Stephen Farlisle was tall and lean against her uncle's bulkier frame, but neither he nor Uncle Oliver were as large as their younger brother. Uncle Maxim was a mountain of a man, tall and broad and when she was little, he could hold her, his daughter Charlotte and her cousin Holly aloft in his arms, giggling as he whirled them about with little effort.

The three brothers stood together, conversing amongst themselves. Holly claimed at one point her father and Davina's had been estranged, and only Uncle Maxim's dramatic return from the dead had brought them to closeness once more. She loved to tease Davina with stories of how her father had wept and wept, but Davina knew better. Her father would never weep where others could see. She knew this to be true, because *she* would never weep where others could see. She felt too much. She knew this. She was her father's daughter, through and through.

Her gaze tripped idly over the guests, noting her mother spoke with her friend Lady Elizabeth, even as she shot heated glances at Davina's father, which he more than returned. Davina quickly averted her gaze. She had no desire to know her parents still lusted after one other.

From the other side of the room, a gentleman stared at her openly.

Brows drawing, she stared back, though *she* at least knew how to disguise her regard. When one tucked themselves away against walls and pillars, one learnt quickly to observe unseen.

She knew, of course, who the gentleman was. Everyone did. Lord Devlin, younger brother of the Marquess of Postleshire. A few years her elder, he was part of a wild set, one that indulged in reckless carriage races and illegal duels over disreputable ladies. Her own brother had spoken longingly of Lord Devlin's exploits, though their father was always quick to remind them such activities were not all fun and games and he had the scars and aches to prove it. When he was a young man, her father had succumbed to wildness in his first few seasons, though it was impossible to imagine her staid, steadfast father as wild as Lord Devlin.

She turned her head. She had no notion why he stared at her so. He was, for want of a better word, beautiful. Chestnut hair perfectly styled, even features, a lush mouth. His shoulders were broad, his hips narrow, his legs long and perfectly framed by his well-tailored trousers. He could have any woman, have her blushing and simpering in moments, and in his arms in minutes.

Davina was not beautiful. She could be termed attractive, she supposed, but only if her maid spent hours styling her hair, even longer applying cosmetics to make it seem as if she wore none, and if she wore garments she found uncomfortable. She much preferred not to bother, and it was probably why she wore the unfashionable gown she now did.

For a while, when she was younger, she'd spent the time on her appearance but honestly, she would much rather the time spent on something—anything—other than that.

"Lady Davina." Somehow he had crossed the room without her notice and stood before her now, a charming smile spread across his handsome features. "May I sit with you?"

She could think of no reason to refuse. "I cannot stop you."

He seemed unaffected by her unenthusiastic response, gracefully arranging himself on the chair beside her. They sat in silence. She was intensely aware of him sitting next to her: the length of his legs, his large hands casually clasping his knees, the smirk twisting his full lips.

"Why are you sad?"

She started and then blushed. *Don't be ridiculous, Davina.* There was no way he knew she had been ogling him. "I beg your pardon?"

"There is a sadness to your smile. Are you sad your cousin is wed?"

Her back snapped straight. "I beg your pardon?" she repeated sharply.

He smirked. "No need to beg."

Jerking her head around, she stared straight ahead and resolved to ignore him.

"I've been watching you."

Still she said nothing.

"You are a very interesting woman to observe."

She snapped her gaze back to him. "Do you find this works?"

He blinked. "I beg your pardon?"

"No need to beg," she countered, and pretended not to notice the quick smile on his pretty mouth. "The mysterious stranger who behaves inappropriately? Do you find ladies swoon at such a manner? Did they put themselves under your spell?"

He regarded her. She refused to quake, meeting his dark gaze with her chin raised. "Usually," he finally said.

Abruptly, she grew tired of his game. "I know of your wager," she said bluntly.

He blinked, and the faintest of frowns touched his brows. "Now I must beg your pardon."

She smiled thinly. "You have wagered with Lord Ingram that you will make me fall in love with you by season's end. It is loathsome, sir, that you would toy with a person's emotions for something as trivial as money."

He was silent a moment, and then, "It is not only money."

"Oh? What, pray tell, is so desirable that you must toy with people's emotions as if you are entitled to do so?"

He shifted uncomfortably.

"Well?"

"The right to say you have won," he mumbled, and then he exhaled forcefully. "You are right."

"I am?" she asked suspiciously.

He nodded slowly. "It *is* loathsome. I did not know how else to—" He exhaled. "I am not...respectable. I cannot approach a lady in a respectable manner."

He—What? Frowning, Davina said, "What does that have to do with your loathsome wager?"

"I—" He closed his eyes, swallowed. When he opened them again, she lost her breath. They were so blue. "It was not only for a wager...that I approached you."

She shook herself. He was wicked. No doubt a hundred women had swooned over that look, the one that made her believe she was his one. His only. "Of course. You are overcome by my beauty."

"No. You are not beautiful."

She blinked. "Is this how you charm your conquests?"

He scowled. "You are not a conquest."

"Your wager would beg to differ," she reminded him.

His scowl darkened, and then cleared. Again, her breath was caught. He was so painfully handsome, and when he looked at her like that, she almost forgot why he had approached her. "Do you know when you are amused, you bite your lip and your eyes light up?"

"I—" She could think of nothing further to say.

His blue eyes almost glowed. "You do not speak overmuch, but when you do, people listen. At a ball, you generally find a seat against wall and lay claim to it, and your cousins drift toward you, pulling up chairs of their own. Your foot taps to the music, but you never accept an invitation to dance. You smile along, and nod your head, and at the end of the ball, you help Lady Demartine to her carriage and then you leave."

She stared at him. He had noticed all that?

The corner of his mouth tilted up. "It was never just the wager."

She...did not know how to respond. Uncertainty wound within her as he regarded her with steady eyes, his gloved hand resting so close to her thigh. "How can I believe you mean anything you say?" she almost whispered.

"You can't," he replied in a hushed tone. "But you know of the wager. I know you know. And there is a time limit."

The mention of the wager put her back on familiar ground. Ground where the fascinating Lord Devlin did not confess he...liked her? "Of course there is," she said sardonically.

He gave a quick grin, acknowledging her tartness. "It is by season's end," he announced grandly.

Her lips twitched. "And so I am to believe if your pursuit remains steadfast beyond the season's end, then your suit is true?"

He nodded judiciously. "Just so." His expression grew serious. "May I call on you tomorrow?"

She regarded him uncertainly. This could not be true. Wicked, wild Lord Devlin could not be interested in her. Not truly. It had to be the wager. Hadn't it?

"Yes," she said, calling herself thrice the fool.

He smiled, wide and genuine, and again he stole her breath.

The next day, he called upon her. And at the next ball, he reserved two of the three waltzes. And the next week he took her riding in the park, the next to a musicale, then to the theatre, and the week after that, he kissed her in Vauxhall Gardens. A fortnight after that, they did more than kiss in a darkened library. And, when the season had ended and he had lost the wager, she asked him to marry her.

And he said yes.

Author's Note

Here we are, at the end of the Lost Lords series.

I can't believe it's all over. The series, bar one novella featuring Lady Violet and the Duke of Meacham, is all over red rover. The Lost Lords have been part of my life for so long now, but I'm so glad the brothers have found their happily ever afters and are living their #bestlives with their lady loves.

Thank you to the amazing AL Brady-Clark for your encouragement and your insight. Couldn't have done it without you.

Thank you to the real Charuni, who made sure I didn't make any egregious mistakes and treated her homeland with the respect Sri Lanka deserves.

I guess it's on with the next! I'm looking to get started with a new series, maybe the 1810 Club featuring Stephen's buddies, or I might dabble in the Spy books I started a while back. I could even go back to the Sisters Charrington books, as I'm dying to tell the tales of Margaret, Kate, and Anna....

Whatever it is, I hope you join me on the journey.

Cassandra

Read the first book in the Lost Lords series

FINDING LORD FARLISLE

The boy she never forgot
Lady Alexandra Torrence knows she's odd. Fascinated by spirits, she sets out to investigate rumours of a ghost at Waithe Hall, the haunt of her childhood. Its shuttered corridors stir her own ghosts: memories of the friend she'd lost. Maxim had been her childhood playmate, her kindred spirit, the boy she was beginning to love …but then he'd abandoned her, only to be lost at sea. She never expected to stumble upon a handsome and rough-hewn man who had made the Hall his home, a man she is shocked to discover is Maxim: alive, older…and with no memory of her.

The girl he finally remembers
Eleven years ago, a shipwreck robbed Lord Maxim Farlisle of his memory. Finally remembering himself, he journeys to his childhood home to find Waithe Hall shut and deserted. Unwilling to face what remains of his family, Maxim makes his home in the abandoned hall only to have a determined beauty invade his uneasy peace. This woman insists he remember her and slowly, he does. Once, he and Alexandra had been inseparable, beloved friends who were growing into something more…but the reasons he left still exist, and how can he offer her a broken man?

As the two rediscover their connection, the promise of young love burns into an overwhelming passion. But the time apart has scarred them both—will they discover a love that binds them together, or will the past tear them apart forever?

Read an Excerpt from
FINDING LORD FARLISLE
Lost Lords, Book One

Chapter One

Northumberland, England, August 1819

LIGHTNING STREAKED ACROSS THE darkening sky and thunder followed. Stillness held sway a moment, the air thick, before a torrent of rain battered the earth.

Wrestling against the wind, Lady Alexandra Torrence tucked her portmanteau closer to her person as she pushed determinedly toward the estate looming in the distance. The storm had been but a sun-shower when she'd set out from Bentley Close, her family's estate only a half hour walk. While the light cloak she wore protected her from the worst of it, the wet was beginning to seep into her skin.

She pulled her cloak tighter. It was only a little farther and she'd be at Waithe Hall, though there would be no one to greet her. Waithe Hall had been closed for years, ever since the previous earl had died. The new earl—Viscount Hudson, as he'd once been—resided almost exclusively in London. Her family and his had been close for as long as she could remember, their townhouses bordering each other in London just as their estates did here in Northumberland. The earl was her elder by nine years, and his brother Stephen by five, but Maxim, the youngest, had been but one year her senior and—

She stopped that thought in its tracks.

Before too much longer, she stood at the entrance to Waithe Hall, and with it, shelter. The huge wooden doors were shut. She could not recall that she had ever seen them closed and locked. In the past when she'd visited the family had been in residence so she would walk straight in, calling for Maxim before she'd completely cleared the entrance—

Slowly, she exhaled. After a moment, she pulled the key from her pocket, the one Maxim had given to her for safekeeping when he was ten and she nine, so they could always find their way back in should the doors ever be locked—

Shoving the key into the lock, she blinked fiercely as she forced memory aside once more. She could do this. It had been years, the wound so old it should have long since faded. She could investigate Waithe Hall and its ghosts, and she would not think of him.

The key turned easily, the door swinging open. She stepped inside. Cavernous silence greeted her, the din of the rain that had been so deafening now distant. The entrance stretched before her, disappearing into darkness, and the storm had made the late afternoon darker than usual, swallowing any light that peeked through closed doors. Pausing mid-step, she wondered if perhaps she had made a mistake in coming here.

Shaking off doubt, she started through the hall. The rain echoed through the vastness, the hollow sound strange after being caught in its fury. Fumbling through her portmanteau she found a candle and tinder.

The flickering light revealed an entrance corridor that opened into an enclosed court encompassing the first and second floors, and an impressive chandelier draped in protective cloth hung at its centre. Memory painted it with crystal and candles, and she remembered sitting on the landing of the second floor, legs dangling through the gaps between balusters as she and Maxim counted the crystals for the hundredth time.

Bowing her head, she cursed herself. She should have known she could not keep the memories at bay.

A roll of thunder reverberated around her, leaving behind quiet and dark. All her memories of Waithe Hall were full of life, the butler directing servants, fresh flowers in the vases lining the court, light spilling through from the mammoth windows. Now the windows were shuttered, and an eerie silence broken only by the sounds of the storm pervaded.

Hitching her bag, she made her way to the sitting room. It was as still as the rest of the estate, the furniture draped in holland covers, the windows also shuttered. Setting her candle down, she placed her cloak over the back of a chair and rested her bag on its seat, glancing nervously about. She caught herself. *Don't be stupid, Alexandra. There's none here.*

Before she could think further, she unbuttoned her bodice. Her clothes were soaked, uncomfortably damp against her skin, and a chill was beginning to seep through, though it was the tail end of summer and the days were still mostly warm. She'd chosen a simple gown, one she knew she could get into and out of herself.

Heat rose on her cheeks as she shucked out of the bodice. There was none here. She *knew* there was no one. Cheeks now burning, she untied her skirt and petticoats, left only in her stays and chemise. She would love to remove her stays as well, but they were only slightly damp and she couldn't bring herself to disrobe more than she had.

Opening her bag, she pulled out a spare bodice, skirt, petticoats and, finally, a towel. Thanking her stars she'd had the forethought to bring it, she quickly swiped herself, chanting all the while there was no one watching her, that doing this in an abandoned sitting room was *not* immodest.

In record time, she'd managed to reclothe herself. Hanging her wet clothes to dry, she pushed her hair out of her face. Once she had explored further, she would choose one of the bedchambers as her base, but for right now the sitting room would suffice.

A thread of guilt wound through her. Technically, the earl did not know she was a guest of Waithe Hall—and by technically, she meant he didn't know at all. She was confident however, he could have no objection. She had been a regular presence at Waithe Hall when she was a girl, and the earl held some affection for her. She was almost positive. Maxim had often said his brother thought her—

Damnation. Bracing herself against a chair, she bowed her head. She had thought more of him in the last hour than she had in the year previous. It was this place. She'd managed to convince herself she no longer felt the sharp bite of grief, but she did. It struck her at odd moments, and she could never predict when. One would think it would have lessened with time, but it hit her fresh and raw, as if she bled all over again. She'd been a fool to think she would remain unaffected returning here—he was everywhere.

She closed her eyes as realisation cut through her. She was going to think of him. It was inevitable. However, she had come here with purpose and she would not allow this preoccupation to deter her.

The ghosts of Waithe Hall beckoned.

A darkening gloom shrouded the drawing room. Night approached, quicker than she'd liked, but she was determined to at least do a preliminary sweep of the estate to refresh her memory before it became too dark to continue. There was much to do before she camped out in the affected room one night soon, not the least of which was determining *which* room was affected.

From her bag, she pulled a compass, a ball of twine, and her notebook. Bending over the flickering light of her candle, she opened her notebook and dated the page, jotting down her notes on the expedition thus far.

There had always been tales of ghosts at Waithe Hall. On her and Maxim's frequent rides about the estate, she remembered listening wide-eyed as Timmons had told them tales of ghosts and woe. The groom had waxed lyrical on the myths and legends of spiritual activity at Waithe Hall, and she'd been completely fascinated. Maxim had never seemed interested, but he'd always followed when she'd concocted a new adventure to discover ghosts and ghouls. As an adult, she'd turned her fascination into a hobby, researching and cataloguing ghost tales at every manor and estate she'd attended. Her own family's estate held a ghost or two, stories her father had been only too happy to tell. She'd documented his tale and others, and had submitted several articles to the Society for the Research of Psychical Phenomena. They hadn't as yet chosen to publish any of them, but she was convinced if she persisted, eventually they would.

Then, four months ago, reports had crossed the earl's desk in London of strange lights at Waithe Hall. He'd mentioned it in passing to her father, who in turn, knowing her fascination, had mentioned it to her. He'd also issued a stern warning she was not to pursue an investigation but, well, she was twenty-five years old and in possession of an inheritance a great aunt had left her. Her father could suggest, but he could not compel.

The lights could be any number of things, but the report had contained accounts of a weeping woman, and the light had become a search light. Memory reminded her of a tale Timmons had told, the lament of a housekeeper of Waithe Hall who had lost a set of keys and caused a massacre. Her lips quirked. Timmons' tales had ever been grisly.

Determination had firmed and within a week she'd made her way to Northumberland and Waithe Hall. Bentley Close had been shut as well, but unlike Waithe Hall, a skeleton staff kept the estate running. Along with her maid, Alexandra had arrived late last night though she hadn't been in a position to set out for Waithe Hall until late this afternoon. Her plan had always been to spend a few days here, but the rain made it that she now had no choice.

She would rather be here than in London anyway. Besides pretending she was unaffected by those who called her odd, her younger sister had finally made her debut at the grand old age of twenty. Lydia was taking society by storm, determined to wring every ounce of pleasure out of her season, and she had confidently informed their parents she didn't intend to wed until she had at least three seasons behind her. At first horrified, their parents had resigned themselves to neither of their daughters marrying any time soon.

As the eldest of her parents' children and a female besides, she had borne the brunt of their expectations in that respect, but at least Harry had now brought them some joy. He and Tessa Pike were to marry next year, the wedding of the heir to a marquessate and a duke's daughter already touted as the event of the season. George had absconded to the continent, no doubt investigating the most macabre medical reports he could, while Michael was still at Eton.

Upstairs, a door slammed shut. Alexandra jumped, hand flying to her racing heart. It was the wind. It had to be. Even now it howled outside, rain pelting the roof and echoing through the hall as distant thunder rolled.

Hugging the notebook to her chest, she shucked off any concerns. There was no time like the present. She would start with an examination of the ground floor. The kitchens and servants rooms would take an age, so better to examine the family rooms and save the servants for another time.

The portrait gallery was as she remembered, a long stretch of hall that displayed the Farlisles in all their permutations. Quickly, she traversed its length, telling herself the dozens of eyes of previous Farlisles did not follow her, that they did not judge her an unwelcome guest. Cold slid up her spine and she moved faster, especially as she passed the portrait of the old earl and his sons, Maxim staring solemnly from the portrait.

Pretending she felt not a skerrick of unease, she noted the gallery's dimensions in her diary and moved on to the second sitting room. Again, nothing in particular was out of the ordinary.

The library was at the end of the corridor, and the door opened easily under her hand. It really was most obliging of the steward not to have locked any of the doors inside the estate. This room was vastly different to her remembrance. Few books lined the shelves thick with dust, and holland covers draped most of the furniture, although one of the high-backed arm chairs before the fire was lacking the covering. Peculiarly, one of the windows here was unshuttered, the weak light of storm-dampened twilight casting eerie shadows on the wall opposite.

She'd always loved the library and its two storeys containing rows upon rows of books. As children, she'd insisted she and Maxim spend an inordinate amount of time within its walls, happily miring herself in book after book. Maxim had always been bored within seconds, spending his time tossing his ever-present cricket ball higher and higher in the air to see if he could hit the ceiling two floors above. He'd even managed it, a time or two.

Sharp pain lodged beneath her breast. Rubbing at her chest, she took a breath against it, pulling herself to the present. Somehow, night had encroached upon the room. How long had she been stood there, lost in memory?

Moving further into the room, she trailed her fingers over the side table next to the undraped chair. A stack of thick books was piled high, the top one containing a marker. Why was there a stack of books? Had an apparition placed them there?

A prickle rippled along her skin. She'd never seen a ghost. She'd heard hundreds, thousands of stories, but she'd never— Steadying herself, she flipped open the book to the spot marked, noting it was a history of the Roman invasion and settlement of Cumbria. Sections and rows were underlined with pencil, writing filled the margins, and there was something about the hand….

Closing the book, she placed it back on the stack. Why was this here? Every other part of Waithe Hall she'd seen had been closed, shut away. This room held an uncovered chair, a stack of books and.... The fireplace held recent ashes.

Her heart began to pound.

Again, something—a door?—banged. Whirling around, she searched the encroaching dark, her gaze desperate as her chest heaved. What if the lights weren't a ghost? What if it was a vagrant, someone dangerous and unkind? What if...what if it were a *murderer*?

The agitated sound of her breathing filled the room. Getting a hold of herself, she reined in her imaginations. Her thoughts could—and frequently did—run to the extreme. Although these anomalies were curious, there could be a perfectly mundane reason for their presence. There was nothing out of the ordinary, besides the books, and the fireplace, and—

She took a breath. *Calm, Alexandra.* She was purportedly an investigator. She would investigate.

The fireplace had without doubt been used recently. Newly cut logs placed in a neat pile to the side. Sconces held half-used candles, their wicks blackened and bodies streaked with melted wax. She could see no other signs of occupation—

Something banged for a third time, closer now, and brought with it a howling wind. Alexandra jumped, grabbing at the table for balance as the door to the library flew open, the heavy wood banging against the wall, the books wobbling and threatening to fall. Blood pounding in her ears, she looked to the darkened maw of the library's entrance.

An indistinct white shape filled the door, hovering at least five feet above the floor.

A scream lodged in her throat. She couldn't move, couldn't make a sound. She could only stare as the thing approached.

Lightning crashed, flashing through the room. She gasped, a short staccato sound that did little to unlock her chest.

Lightning crashed again. The shape became distinct in the brief flash of light, revealing a man dressed in shirt sleeves and breeches, his dark hair long about his harsh face. A strong, handsome face that held traces of the boy she'd thought never to see again.

Blood drained from her own face, such she felt faint. "Maxim?"

Chapter Two

"WHAT ARE YOU DOING here?" it—he—growled.

"Maxim?" she repeated stupidly. The apparition before her looked so much like Maxim...if Maxim had grown to a man, developed an abundance of muscle and four inches of height. It couldn't be Maxim...but if it were an apparition, why would he appear grown? When last she'd seen him, he'd been fifteen and skinny as a reed, not much taller than she. It couldn't be him.

Lightning lit the room once more. His shirt was loose about his thighs, the ties undone and the neck gaping open, his breeches smudged with dirt. All was well tailored and untattered. Surely, if he were a ghost, his raiments should be tattered?

The same chestnut hair fell over his brow, too long and ragged, while his face had broadened and hardened, his eyes were the same, chocolate brown under dark brows. He'd grown to a man, broad shoulders and ropy muscle apparent behind the scant clothes he wore, his breeches stretched over powerful thighs and strong calves, his large feet shod in well-worn leather boots.

He was supposed to be dead. Eleven years ago, he had abruptly left Eton and set sail on one of the Roxwaithe ships, bound for America. She'd been so confused at the time, and he'd refused to tell her why. Six months later, they had received word the ship had been lost at sea. None had survived.

With startling clarity, she remembered that day. Her father's face, careworn and concerned, as he'd told her. Her mother's worried eyes. The pain in her chest, frozen at first, until she'd excused herself, blindly making her way to her chamber only to stand in its centre, confusion filling her until she'd happened to glance upon his cricket ball, the one he'd given her the last time she'd seen him, where he'd been worried about something but he'd refused to tell her what and yelled at her when she'd pressed him, and once she'd returned home she'd thrown it onto her dressing table, angry beyond belief at him, and then, then a great gaping hole had cracked open inside her and she'd slid to the floor, pain and grief and devastation growing inside her until it had encompassed all, it had encompassed everything and it hadn't stopped, it hadn't stopped, it—

It was eleven years ago. The pain had faded, but never truly left. She'd thought she'd learned to live with it. But now…he was here?

A thunderous scowl on his face, he made a noise of impatience. "I do not have the inclination for this, girl. Tell me why you have come."

His voice crashed over her. That, too, had deepened with age, but it was him. It was him.

"It is you." Joy filled her, so big it felt her skin couldn't contain it. Throwing herself at him, she enveloped him in a hug.

He stiffened.

Embarrassment coursed through her. What was she thinking? Immediately, she untangled herself from him. "I beg your pardon," she stammered. Always before they'd been exuberant in their affections. They'd always found ways to touch one another, even though that last summer, the one before he'd gone away, she'd begun to feel...more.

Clasping her hands before her, she brought herself to the present. Much had changed, now they were grown and he, apparently, had not died.

Maxim had not died.

A wave of emotion swept her, a mix of relief, joy, incredulity…. It buckled her knees and burned her eyes. He was alive. Maxim was alive.

"When did you return? Do your brothers know?" she asked, steadying herself as she swiped at the wetness on her cheeks. "The earl is lately in London, but I'm certain he would return should he know. My father will be so pleased to see, as will my mother. George and Harry will be beside themselves, and Lydia and Michael too, though they were so young when—" She cut herself off, barely able to say the word died. "We mourned you, Maxim."

He came closer. He'd grown so tall. When last she'd seen him, barely an inch had separated them, but now he was at least two hands taller. Faint lines fanned from his eyes, the tanned skin shocking in the cold English weather. Wherever he'd been, it had been sunburned.

"I ask again," he said. "Why have you come?"

Confusion drew her brows. "Maxim? Don't you remember me?"

Starting at the blonde hair piled limply on her head thanks to the rain, he ran his gaze over her. He traced her face, her throat, travelled over her chest, swept her legs. A tingling began within her, gathering low. She was suddenly aware of how her breasts pushed against the fabric of her chemise with every breath, of a pulse between her legs that beat slow, steady….

He raised his gaze to hers. Silence filled the space between them before, succinctly, "No."

It was like a punch to her belly. "It's me. Alexandra."

No reaction.

Oh. Oh, this hurt.

Lifting her chin, she managed, "I am Lady Alexandra Torrence, daughter of your neighbour, the Marquis of Demartine. We grew up together."

His expression did not change.

"Your father, the previous earl, and mine were like brothers."

He stared at her. "Previous earl?" he finally asked.

"Yes," she said. "Your father passed away some years ago. Your eldest brother is now earl."

Again, no change in expression. Did he not care his father had died? But what did she know of this new Maxim? Less than an hour ago, she had not known he was alive.

He continued to stare at her. She fought the urge to shift under that flat gaze. "Why are you here?" he repeated, his tone harsh and impatient.

"I was—" Her voice cracked. Cursing her nerves, she cleared her throat. "I am investigating. The villagers spoke of a ghostly presence, lights and wails, and I…." She trailed off. Lord, it made her sound so odd. He'd always teased her about that oddness, and always with affection. She didn't know what this new Maxim would do.

Finally there was expression on his face. She wished it had remained stony. "Ghosts? You have invaded my home for ghosts?"

The disgust in his voice made her cringe. "To be fair, I didn't know you were here. No one did."

Expression still disdainful, he didn't reply.

Irritation pushed aside devastation. How could he not remember her? "This is not your home."

His brows shot up. "That is your argument?"

He sounded so much like her Maxim. They'd argued often, and the number of times he'd said those exact words, in that exact tone.... She shook herself. "Yes. It is."

"A fallacy. You argue a fallacy."

"It is not a fallacy. It is objectively true. Waithe Hall is the ancestral seat of the Earls of Roxwaithe. You are not the Earl of Roxwaithe, ergo, it is not your home." Knowing it was childish, she tossed her hair and glared.

Crossing his arms, he scowled. "I know you are somewhere you don't belong."

"So are you," she pointed out.

"This is my family home."

"It's your brother's," she said. "You're being deliberately obtuse."

"And you're being obstinate."

"I'm being obstinate? Me?" This was such a ridiculous argument, and yet it was familiar. They'd argued like this all the time, and he was reacting exactly as her Maxim would react, and—

Stepping forward, he deliberately loomed over her. "I come into my library to find a trespasser, poking around in my things."

"Waithe Hall is shut. Roxwaithe hasn't been here in years. No one is supposed to be here. You aren't even supposed to be alive. How are you even feeding yourself?"

Pinching the bridge of his nose, he shook his head. "Why am I arguing with you? You're a trespasser I don't know."

Rage, such as she'd never experienced before, exploded. How dare he? How dare he pretend not to know her? Her fingers curled into fists and she told herself she could not punch him. She was a lady, and he was a clodpole. "Don't be stupid."

He stilled, and something flickered in his dark eyes. "You will leave the way you came."

"With pleasure," she snapped. Pushing past him, she stalked from the library, through the entrance hall, and wrenched the door open. Rain pelted her, almost horizontal as the wind howled and lightning crashed across the sky. She plunged into it, anger propelling her even as she was drenched in moments.

She'd not gotten more than two strides before a large hand grabbed her shoulder and hauled her back inside. Maxim slammed the door shut and shook himself, water falling to the marble floor. "Do you have any brains?" he demanded.

"You told me to go. I have no desire to say here with you."

"You wouldn't get half a mile before you'd catch your death. You'll stay here."

"It would not be proper," she said stiffly.

He laughed harshly. "Hunting a ghost is not proper, either. You will stay here."

Mutinously, she glared at him. Damnation. She could not even argue that point. Belatedly, she realised the rain had plastered his shirt to his body, clinging to hard muscle and broad shoulders.

Mouth abruptly dry, her breath locked in her chest.

He didn't seem to notice her distraction. "Come," he said, holding aloft a lamp he'd magically produced, before turning on his heel to stride down the corridor. Hesitantly, she followed.

They wound through the Hall, climbing the grand stairs and making their way to the family apartments, the corridors she remembered from her—their—childhood. Wrapping her arms about herself, she cursed herself at the soaked fabric. She'd only brought two gowns, and now both were wet.

He halted before a door. "You may stay here," he said, pushing it open.

Passing him, she entered a bedchamber, again with most of the furniture covered. The bed, though, was not, holding a mattress along with pillows and sheets.

Surprise filled her. "Is this where you sleep?"

He placed the lamp on the dresser. "Goodnight."

"Good—?" He was gone before she finished the word.

Wrapping her arms about her torso, she stopped herself from rushing after him. She wanted to assure herself she hadn't imagined him, that he was real, that he was alive…and she needed to get her bag, she had a nightgown and a change of underclothes, and—Maxim was alive.

Legs giving out, she collapsed onto the bed. The bed he had slept in, unmade with the sheets rucked to the foot of the bed. A faint scent wound about her, woodsy and indistinct, but she knew it was his, knew it was Maxim's. A harsh sob broke from her, and another, eleven years of emotion exploding. Sliding from the bed, she pulled herself into a ball, hot forehead against her updrawn knees, her cheeks wet, her chest hurting, her sodden clothes feeling as if they weighed a hundred pounds.

The wind howled, rain pelting the window. They'd all thought him dead. She'd thought him dead. Her dearest companion, her best friend. Maxim.

Slowly, her sobs subsided. She couldn't stay here. She couldn't take his bed from him, and she.... She wanted to know. She wanted to know everything. Why was he here? Why hadn't he gone to his brothers? Why was he lurking in Waithe Hall alone? When had he returned?

Did he really not remember her?

Taking a shuddering breath, she wiped at her cheeks. She needed to know and surely he would tell her. Even if he didn't remember her.

Rising to her feet, she squared her shoulders. Well, she would make him remember her...and then she would make him let her hug him.

Read the second book in the Lost Lords series

RESCUING LORD ROXWAITHE

The girl he's always loved
Oliver, Earl of Roxwaithe, has always regarded Lady Lydia Torrence as a sibling even as she'd declared one day they would wed. Fourteen years her elder, Oliver was convinced Lydia felt only a crush and when she inevitably declared her love, he had to refuse. After she left for the Continent, he told himself he didn't miss her, that she had always been too young, and if perhaps he'd noticed she had become a woman, that was best left unsaid.

The man she's always adored
Lydia had always known she loved Oliver and he loved her. Furious he would claim she was too young, she determined to take the Continent by storm, to hone her skills and become an expert in flirtation. Upon her return to London, she'd show him she was a fully-grown woman who knew what she wanted—and she wanted him.

Oliver is stubborn in his resolve until a new suitor for Lydia puts Oliver's resolve to the test. Will he discover the girl he's always loved has become the woman he will forever adore?

Read a novella set in the Lost Lords world

PERSUADING LADY PENELOPE

After years out of Society, Lady Penelope Masterton is eager to enjoy her friend's house party. Ever the wallflower, she never expects to attract any attention, especially not the attention of the Earl Wainwright. Everyone says he's an inconstant flirt, that no lady has ever held his regard for longer than a season, so why, then, does the roguishly handsome earl claim he wants her for his wife?

Alastair, Earl Wainwright, thought he would never find his person, the one he would love and cherish above all others, and he certainly never expected to find her at Lady Stayne's house party. His first sight of Lady Penelope takes his breath and then his heart, but a reputation for inconstancy makes it she doesn't believe his suit is true.

Now, Wainwright is desperate to do everything he can to convince Penelope he is worth taking a chance…and that a never-serious rogue can be deadly serious about persuading his lady.

TEACH ME

Ever curious, Elizabeth, Viscountess Rocksley, has turned her curiosity to erotic pleasure. Three years a widow, she boldly employs the madam of a brothel for guidance but never had she expected her education to be conducted by a coldly handsome peer of the realm.

To the Earl of Malvern, the erotic tutelage of a skittish widow is little more than sport, however the woman he teaches is far from the mouse he expects. With her sly humor and insistent joy, Elizabeth obliterates all his expectations and he, unwillingly fascinated, can't prevent his fall.

Each more intrigued than they are willing to admit, Elizabeth and Malvern embark upon a tutelage that will challenge them, change them, come to mean everything to them…until a heartbreaking betrayal threatens to tear them apart forever.

SILK & SCANDAL
THE SILK SERIES, BOOK 1

Eight years ago...
Thomas Cartwright and Lady Nicola Fitzgibbons were friends. Over the wall separating their homes, Thomas and Nicola talked of all things – his studies to become a barrister, her frustrations with a lady's limitations.

All things end.
When her diplomat father gains a post in Hong Kong, Nicola must follow. Bored and alone, she falls into scandal. Mired in his studies of the law and aware of the need for circumspection, Thomas feels forced to sever their ties.

But now Lady Nicola is back…and she won't let him ignore her.

ROUGH DIAMOND
The Diamond Series, Book 1

Owner of the Diamond Saloon and Theater, Alice Reynolds is astounded when a fancy Englishman offers to buy her saloon. She won't be selling her saloon to anyone, let alone a man with a pretty, empty-headed grin...but then, she reckons that grin just might be a lie, and a man of intelligence and cunning resides beneath.

Rupert Llewellyn has another purpose for offering to buy the pretty widow's saloon—the coal buried deep in land she owns. However, he never banked on her knowing eyes making him weak at the knees, or how his deception would burn upon his soul.

Each determined to outwit the other, they tantalize and tease until passion explodes. But can their desire bridge the lies told and trust broken?

About Cassandra Dean

Cassandra Dean is an award-winning author of historical and fantasy romance. She grew up daydreaming, inventing fantastical worlds and marvellous adventures. Once she learned to read (First phrase – To the Beach. True story), she was never without a book, reading of other people's fantastical worlds and marvellous adventures.

Cassandra is proud to call South Australia her home, where she regularly cheers on her AFL football team and creates her next tale.

Connect with Cassandra

cassandradean.com

facebook.com/AuthorCassandraDean

twitter.com/authorCassDean

instagram.com/authorcassdean

bookbub.com/authors/cassandra-dean

To learn about exclusive content, upcoming releases and giveaways,
join Cassandra's mailing list:

cassandradean.com/extras/subscribe

Printed in Great Britain
by Amazon